Connections
A Jack Contino
Crime Story

Connections

by

Steven P. Marini

Gypsy Shadow Publishing

Connections
by
Steven P. Marini

All rights reserved
Copyright © July 20, 2012, Steven P. Marini
Cover Art Copyright © 2012, Charlotte Holley

Gypsy Shadow Publishing, LLC
Lockhart, TX
www.gypsyshadow.com

    Names, characters and incidents depicted in this book are products of the author's imagination, or are used fictitiously. Any resemblance to actual events, locales, organizations, or persons, living or dead, is entirely coincidental and beyond the intent of the author or the publisher.

    No part of this book may be reproduced or shared by any electronic or mechanical means, including but not limited to printing, file sharing, and email, without prior written permission from Gypsy Shadow Publishing, LLC.

Library of Congress Control Number: 2012948028
eBook ISBN: 978-1-61950-094-6
Print ISBN: 978-1-61950-108-9

Published in the United States of America

First eBook Edition: July, 2012
First Print Edition: August, 2012

Praise for Connections

"Fast paced and suspenseful . . . Skillfully constructed . . . the perfect blending of characters, action and drama gives the reader topnotch entertainment . . . The perfect read for a weekend of enjoyment. . . ."

—Tom Farrell
Massachusetts State Police (Ret)

"A dash of Chandler, a dab of Hammet and a fast paced narrative that will keep you glued to the page. CONNECTIONS is a roller-coaster ride into Boston's past, complete with snappy dialogue, engaging characters and an intriguing plot. If you like crime novels that seamlessly blend violence, sex, and action, this is your kind of novel."

—Arlene Kay
Author of INTRUSION

DEDICATION

To my wife and partner, Louise, and my children: Lisa, Nick and Andrea. You make my world.

Acknowledgements

Tom Leary, Chief, Needham, MA, Police Department, retired, for his valuable consultation regarding police procedure.
Beth Ann Weymer Rossi, for her help in the very early stages. Always a teacher.
Anne Speyer, Allyson Peltier and Rus VanWestervelt, for helping me grow as a writer.

Prologue

Jack Contino was a natural cop. It never bothered him to face a dangerous situation. He had size, strength and brains; good elements for police work. He was a combat vet from World War II, and he saw hell in the Pacific theater. If you've been to hell once, it toughens you up for future visits. Cops visit hell often.

It was 1945 and Jack was in his second year with the Metropolitan District Commission Police, often called the METS, walking foot patrol on a sunny Saturday afternoon at Nantasket Beach with another young officer, Leo Barbado.

"Summer is upon us, big fellow," said Leo. "This place can get crazy if the crowds get too big."

"That's why we're here, to protect the people from themselves, especially at the amusement park."

"Why would anybody want to ride that rickety looking old roller coaster?"

"A lot of reasons, I guess, but some folks just need a thrill."

"Not me. This job will provide plenty of thrills for years to come, I'm sure."

"Is that why you became a cop, Leo, for the thrills?"

"Yeah, and the money. Don't forget the money. Why did you become a cop, Jack?"

"Well, I actually enjoyed the army life when I first went in; the discipline, the order, the authority to enforce the rules. I think law enforcement offers much of that."

"Authority, aka power, and carrying a gun. Just kidding, Jack."

"Hey, I believe a lot of our colleagues go into police work for those very reasons. Not me. If that's all you got going for you, it's not going to mean much to you in the long run. Leo, after Pearl, I wanted to protect America, like everybody else. But while overseas, I saw that the Asian people needed help, too. There was a lot of poverty, disease, starvation, you name it, among the people we were supposed to hate. They struggled just to get by every day. I realized people here at home have daily struggles, too."

"Yes, I know. I'm struggling to get somewhere with that waitress I've been dating."

"You're a bundle of laughs, buddy boy. I'm not trying to get preachy, but I mean it. We can help people work through the tough times at home by helping to keep some order in this little universe. Most of the people at this place today are here to have fun and forget their troubles. But you know there are some jerks who want to cause trouble: pickpockets, drunks, tough guys showing off. That's why we're here, too."

"I guess you're right, Jack. I just hope those bastards will give us a break today. Maybe they'll hold off until the night shift comes on."

"That's fine by me, cowboy, but don't count on it."

As Jack finished his words, they heard the sound of glass shattering. The cops looked at each other without speaking. It could be a dropped bottle by a tired worker at the food tent. It could be a drunken guy making a public nuisance. It could be a lot of things, but whatever, it needed the police to check it out.

Chapter One
September 1974

  Jack Contino always walked into a bar like he owned the place. He sucked in his gut as best he could before entering, keeping his six-foot four inch, two-hundred and thirty pound frame as erect as a fifty-four-year-old veteran cop could. Despite his size, Jack had a lot of spring in his step. It was late afternoon in Boston, the right time to catch one of the parking spots vacated by the daily commuter students, who gobbled them up by seven in the morning. Jack worked his way onto an open stool at the far end of the bar and casually surveyed the room.

  The Bullpen entrance was two steps down at the end of a short sidewalk on Commonwealth Avenue across from Boston University. Its patrons were both working class and B.U. students, mostly the older ones taking classes through the Metropolitan College. Some classes started as early as four-thirty. Winter was over, but people still wore warm clothing. Some liked to get ready for class with a cold one. A long, L-shaped oak bar took up the left side of the room. Tables with four chairs each were scattered along the right, leaving a small passage to the bar. The lighting was dim and got dimmer toward the back.

  The first two tables were occupied by a small group of university employees, a young mix of males and females. They were a bit loud and seemed to be enjoying themselves. There were five men at the bar. Two looked like groundskeepers, with their heavy work boots and cuffed work pants and the others might be faculty or grad students. The working men looked to be about forty plus while the others were probably in their late twenties. Casual conversation swirled among the three faculty/grad types. Jack couldn't make out what the working men were saying to each other. He noticed a lone figure sitting at a table in the back corner, a man about his own age. The man was wearing a shiny Red Sox jacket and a blue baseball cap with a big red *B* on the front above the visor. A hamburger plate with fries sat in front of him, but he was looking around more than eating. His beer bottle was half empty. He knew Jack had spotted him.

"Give me two bottles of Miller," said Jack, as the bartender approached. She was a middle aged woman wearing a white blouse buttoned up to the neck and black slacks. About five-foot six, she cut a nice figure, her long brown hair in a ponytail.

"Coming right up."

Jack put some bills on the bar when the beers arrived. He stood up with one in each hand and walked over to the guy in the corner. He placed a bottle in front of the man seated with his back to the wall and slid into the chair against the other wall. Both men had a view of the whole room. Jack took a swig from his bottle.

"So, you got yourself into a tight little spot in Connecticut," said Jack. That served as an introduction.

"Yeah, well, it was supposed to be a good deal, but it didn't go so good. That's why I called your office. I need some help and I've heard some talk that you're the guy for that. The word is you're a straight up guy. You gotta help me out, Jack. You work with the Feds. You can pull some strings." He took a bite of his burger, as if to cue Jack.

"You think I'm the Seventh Cavalry coming to your rescue? You ran some guns to guys planning a bank job in Hartford. What the hell were you thinking? Now the Feds have your number." Jack swigged his beer.

"Hey, I didn't know what they were planning. And those pieces can't be traced to me. I made sure of that. The Feds are setting me up. Whatever they claim to have is bogus."

"Hey, keep calm, will you? Regardless of what you think is happening, let me tell you what *is* happening. The FBI has you targeted, and they have a way of making life miserable for people in their crosshairs. You ran the guns to a guy who moved them to another party, the guys who wanted the bank. Lucky for you they never got to the gig, because if they had, you'd already be in lock up and I couldn't be of much help to you. But your guy wants to go home at night, so he gave you up. They already have enough to put you away, Charlie."

"So why didn't they?"

Jack sat back and smiled a big smile, the kind that says *I'm your Daddy*. He helped himself to a couple of fries and washed them down with beer.

"I'm already helping you out, get it? But I'm not a social worker. You have to make it worth my while."

"What can I do?" "It's time for you to reconsider this omerta crap, your code of silence. I know you're in a good position to know a lot about what the Boston is doing. We know about that North End apartment of yours. It attracts some interesting people. Oh, don't look so surprised. We've heard about it now and then. Some solid information from you, stuff that will hold up in court, might make me willing to talk to the Feds on your behalf. I'm especially interested in the Winter Hill guys. There's one guy I'd really like to nail. He's got connections at the State House, so he thinks he's bullet proof."

"Hey, Jack. I don't want to go there. Are you nuts? I'd be asking for a bullet. Hell, a bullet would be merciful the way that guy works."

"He's been pissing me off for a long time, but I've got to be careful. Let's just say he's got good insulation."

"There's a lot of stuff that goes on that's got nothing to do with him. Let's focus on some of that."

"Well, it better be good. Think it over, old boy. Time's a wastin'."

Jack took a long drink from his beer. He pushed back from the table, got up and walked away. The other guy sat, silently watching Jack leave. He had some decisions to make. He couldn't see the broad smile on Jack's face.

Chapter Two
1947

In 1947, after working with the Metropolitan District Commission Police for over two years, Jack Contino started taking day classes at Walker College, a small junior college in his hometown of Somerville. He didn't mind working the night beat, the standard practice for new police officers, but he knew he wanted to get off the graveyard shift and make detective. An Associate's degree in Criminal Justice would help him advance.

A park with a large lawn area was located just across the street from the three Victorian houses that comprised the college, an administration building and two classroom buildings. Jack liked to bring a muffin and a thermos with coffee to the park before class and enjoy some peaceful time after patrolling all night. There were park benches to get off his feet. On this particular morning, a lovely young woman who he had seen on other mornings already occupied Jack's favorite bench. That was interesting.

"Excuse me, but do you mind if I sit here?" he asked.

"No, not at all." Jack knew his size and physique impressed women, but he didn't let it go to his head. He saw interest in her eyes.

Jack sat down, poured some coffee into the cup that covered the thermos and took a sip. The flavor was something he had been waiting for. It was probably obvious.

"Tough night?" she asked, still looking into the textbook she held in front of her.

Jack showed a wry smile. "Naw, not so bad. Just long, that's all. I work nights."

She closed her book and slipped it into a green bag with a long drawstring, then stood up clutching the bag in front of her. "Enjoy your breakfast."

Jack watched her walk away. He liked the swooshing sound her Florence Nightingale dress made as she walked. He was impressed with the nurses he had met while in the Army. They had guts working in combat zones. He hoped this one would never have such an experience.

Their morning meetings became more frequent and their conversations grew longer each morning. Her name was Natalie Buono, a first year nursing student, who took the bus over from her parent's house in Medford. Jack was hooked.

On this morning, Natalie spoke first. "What was it like, Jack, being stationed at Pearl when they attacked?"

"It was awful. We couldn't believe what was happening. I mean, it was a quiet Sunday morning and then all of a sudden all hell broke loose. Excuse me, I mean it got real nasty."

"That's okay, Jack. I'm a big girl."

Jack paused a moment. "It's such a shame that all happened. I mean, Pearl was good duty up 'til then. The Army was not so bad. I even did a little boxing."

"I'll bet you were good at it."

"Yes, I was. Not too many guys wanted to fight me after a while, so I just gave it up. I fought heavyweight."

"Well, I'm glad you came out all right, otherwise this would be a difficult conversation."

Jack checked his schedule for his off-duty days and began taking Natalie out to dinner and movies. They dated regularly and those days became the happiest of Jack's life. He had found his love.

After a cold winter, spring finally came in 1948, and Jack was happy to be put on a rotating shift: two days on duty, a day off, two nights on, and then two days off. Usually the new schedule gave him more time to be with Natalie, but sometimes she had studying to do at night and he left her alone with her school work.

One night, Jack and a friend from the force, Leo Barbado, went to a Somerville bar to relax and knock back a few beers.

The first two lagers went down well and Jack enjoyed his conversation with Leo. They ordered another round just about the time the place started to get noisy. Jack's back was to the bar, but Leo could see it clearly. A tall, thin young man was on his feet, arguing with a guy on a bar stool. The seated man held his hand up as if to call a halt to the discussion and he spun around on the stool, turning his back to his adversary.

"Don't turn your back on me, asshole." He backslapped the guy on the head hard.

The guy spun back around. "Hey, I don't want any trouble." He turned his back again.

"Oh, no? Then just pay me what you owe and we'll all be happy." He backslapped the guy again.

Jack was getting irritated at not seeing what was going on, so he turned to see who was having the argument. He turned back to Leo.

"You know him, Jack?"

"I'm afraid I do. Young Tommy Shea, neighborhood tough guy and overall pain in the ass. I went to high school with his older brother, Jimmy. He's an asshole of another kind. This one thinks he can beat up the world. He's already done time in juvy. He's getting on my nerves."

Jack stood up from his table and pushed his chair back.

"Jack, we're off duty."

"I know. This will be strictly unofficial. Stay back unless he's got help. Just me and him."

He approached Shea while Leo looked around the room to see if anybody else got up.

"Hey," he said, getting in Shea's face. "I'm trying to enjoy my beer and you're making it difficult with all this noise. Why don't you take it outside?"

Shea turned and recognized Jack. "Oh, the big tough cop wants me to take it outside. Yeah, I know who you are. Think you're a tough guy 'cause you're a cop. Contino, the wop cop."

Jack swallowed hard and kept quiet. His mother had always taught him to count to ten when he got mad. This time, he didn't make it past five. "Like I said, why don't you take it outside?"

"Why don't you take it outside, wop cop, if you got the balls?"

Jack felt his heart quicken as the anger built. "You know what, Shea? This is my lucky day because I just happen to be off duty. So I'd be happy to get in some fresh air. Why don't you come along?"

In a minute, they were standing in a back parking lot facing each other close up. About half the bar patrons, including Leo, rushed out the door to form a circle around the two fighters. Jack held his fists like a trained boxer. Shea looked like a caged animal about to pounce on whoever opened the cage door.

They inched closer to one another and suddenly Shea threw a fast right fist at Jack's head. He slipped the punch easily. Shea stepped toward Jack and threw another right. Jack deflected that one with his left arm. Then Shea landed a left hook to Jack's midsection. He followed it up by rushing into Jack with his shoulder, hitting Jack in the gut, knocking him back, but not down. He grabbed Jack, wrapping his left arm around him in a clinch. While they tugged at each other, Shea's right hand produced a shard of beer bottle glass from his pants pocket. As Jack pushed him back from the clinch, Shea swung at Jack's face with the glass, grazing the left side of his chin. Blood appeared immediately.

Jack should have expected a less than fair fight from Shea. Okay, no more fooling around. Jack closed in on Shea, who still held the glass shard in his hand. Jack feigned a hard left jab at Shea who reacted by blocking his face with his hands. Like a football placekicker, Jack swung his right foot up at his target with great force. His kick caught Shea in the groin and he buckled over in pain, but stayed on his feet. Jack then hit him with a powerful right to the jaw that staggered Shea. Another right hand to the gut bent Shea over. Jack could have ended it right there with another right. He wanted to kill the punk. Instead, he grabbed Shea's shirt with his left hand and began slapping him repeatedly, open palm, then backhand. There's something about slapping a guy around. It's almost like a parent beating a child.

Jack pushed the groggy Shea to the ground and checked him for weapons. Surprised to find him clean, Jack went back inside with Leo and finished his beer.

"Nice work, Jack. He won't bother you again."

"I think he'll try. But he'll use another angle next time. If he's like his smarter, older brother, he'll always try to get an angle, you know, some advantage over the other guy. And he's just not cut out for the straight life. We're going to hear more from him."

On a bright spring day in June, 1948, Jack entered St. Joseph's Church in Medford through the side door. His buddy from the police force and best man, Leo Barbado, followed behind him. Jack was comfortable in the formal wear for the wedding, but Leo looked like a fish out of water, constantly fidgeting with his necktie and cuffs.

"Relax pal. You'd think you were the one getting married today. You got the rings?"

"Yeah, of course I've got the rings."

"Just making sure. I don't want anything to mess this up for Natalie, you know. Everything's got to go real smooth today."

"Don't worry, Jack. Everything is going to be great. No bad guys today."

The wedding and reception went without a hitch and the happy couple took off for a few honeymoon days on Cape Cod—Only Jack couldn't forget about Tommy Shea.

Chapter Three
October 1974

Maria walked slowly into the kitchen, tightened her robe and poured herself another Dewar's after dropping two ice cubes into her glass. "You want one?" she called to Ben in the living room.

"No. I'm good. Thanks," he replied. "Besides, I've got to go soon." *Yeah*, he thought. *I've got some business to take care of.*

Maria lost her smile. She knew enough about Ben's professional activities to understand that they were sometimes beyond the law. She forced another smile.

"Well, that's my Ben all right. Good old Mr. Hit and Run. Only no hit? C'mon. What's the rush?"

She took a sip from her Scotch and slid down onto the sofa next to him, leaning her head on his shoulder. "It's after 1:00 a.m. That means it's Sunday. I thought you took Sundays off. I'm kind of in the mood for, you know, having you stay." She put her glass down.

"I'll be back later," he said. "I promise."

He swallowed the last drop of Scotch from his glass and pulled himself up from the sofa. Maria let her head slide off Ben and she curled into a ball as he got up. She turned onto her back, pulling her legs up onto the sofa. She placed one hand against her forehead, her fingernails lightly touching her brow.

"Oh, Ben, you just can't leave me. Where shall I go? What shall I do?" she said, mocking the voice of Scarlet O'Hara in *Gone With the Wind*.

Ben finished putting on his dark overcoat and looked at Maria as he reached the door. "Frankly, my dear, I don't—"

"Oh, don't bother. Hey, tell me, what other bad impressions do you do?"

"All my impressions."

He turned to open the door. When he looked back at Maria, who was now standing, she had dropped her robe, showing her perfect body. She looked at Ben with her head to one side, as if making one last offer.

"Scarlet never did that," he said smiling.

She stepped closer, pressing herself against him. "Well, if she had, it would have surely changed the ending to that story."

He leaned toward her, his hand still on the door knob and kissed her. "Nice try, but I still gotta go."

"Oh, poo!"

At this hour, it was a quick drive to Commercial Street. He headed east for a couple of blocks and then steered his 1956 Ford Thunderbird two-seater down an alleyway leading to a small parking area. There were no open parking places, but Ben saw the BMW owned by Charlie *The Senator* Senatori, who owned the building that was his intended destination. He swung his T-Bird around and backed it up to Charlie's Beemer. He shut down the engine and turned to get his tall frame out of the small vehicle. Ben had always liked these classic two-seaters, so he'd bought one a couple of years before and kept it in good running condition. Ben glanced around at the other cars parked in the area. *Nothing that didn't belong,* he thought to himself.

Still wearing his thin driving gloves, Ben reached into his pants pocket and took out a set of keys. He slipped one into the keyhole and let himself into the small hallway leading to the stairs. Ben was one of a handful who had keys to this apartment. Nobody actually lived here. Charlie had acquired the townhouse to use for business transactions and as a hangout.

Ben climbed the carpeted back stairs quietly and opened the door at the top. As he emerged into the first floor hallway, he heard several voices coming from the dining room. He stepped through the open archway into the room, where four familiar faces looked up at him from the round game table. Charlie Senatori was counting out chips and passing them to the players who gave him large amounts of cash.

"I was afraid you were going to crap out on us tonight," said Charlie.

"Who, me? No way. Hey, it's been a while between games. When I heard there was a game on tonight I started to feel lucky."

"That's a good thing, Ben," said one of the players.

It was Fred Di Nardi. Ben knew him from other game nights. Fred owned a small club in The Combat Zone. He was known as a guy who could provide you with a private back room where you could conduct special business without being disturbed; business involving the sale and distribution of certain substances was frowned upon by the DEA.

"We'd sure miss the chance to separate you from your money . . . again!" Fred laughed.

"Cute! Real cute," Ben replied.

Without taking off his coat, Ben went to the corner hutch displaying several bottles of liquor, glasses, a pitcher of water and an ice bucket. He poured himself a Scotch and took a sip. He looked at the other bottles on the hutch. Besides the Dewar's, there was a Glen Fiddich single malt bottle, a Stoli vodka, a Wild Turkey and a Ruffino Chianti. That should keep everyone happy for the night; everyone who was not losing his shirt.

Giani Bertoli came up to the hutch. He grabbed the Glen Fiddich and filled a shot glass. "When are you gonna graduate up to the good stuff, Ben?"

Giani was the elder statesman of this group. He had lived in Boston since he was six, when his parents moved to the United States to get away from the tyranny of Mussolini. His father made his own wine at home, and the son eventually took a deep interest in the liquor business himself. He started working for a beer and wine distributor when he reached his twenties. He learned the business from the bottom up, was good with figures and eventually got his A.A. in Accounting, which, of course, made him the best candidate to take over the bookkeeping duties from the owner, who trusted him completely. That, along with his skill with what one might call the *over and under method* of accounting, enabled Giani to fudge the books to his profit on a regular basis. Giani made a life of betraying trust.

"I'll have to give it a try sometime," said Ben. "But tonight, I'll stick with my Dewar's."

Tom Jacobs looked up from the table at Ben and Giani. He didn't say anything. Tom worked for a Boston newspaper as a street reporter who often covered the Boston underworld. His prime contacts were right in this room. He was particularly friendly with Giani Bertoli, whose friendship he had cultivated over several years. The men saw Tom as a straight shooter who never crossed over the line of their respect and trust when he covered a story. They let him know just enough to get his story printed and to serve their purposes, but he had nothing the police would be interested in, although sometimes they wondered about that. That's how he served the guys, making a news report that, although mostly factual, would send the police down a dark alley.

"Hey, Tom," said Ben. Tom looked at him and nodded. "You know, for a reporter, Tom doesn't talk very much," he said to the whole room. They chuckled and Tom smiled.

"I gotta save it," said Tom.

Everyone but Ben had taken a seat at the table. He put his drink down on the hutch, and Fred noticed Ben was still wearing driving gloves.

"Hey, Ben, what's with the gloves? Trying to not leave fingerprints?"

"Oh, yeah. Always keep the place clean, you know."

Everybody laughed. "Geeze, I just remembered I brought a little surprise for Charlie," said Ben. "I left it in the car. I'll go get it and be right back."

"She'd better be about five foot-two and brunette," said Charlie. Ben smiled at him and hurried out of the room and down the back stairs.

Ben went out to his car, a move designed to make his deception credible, and took a new, 1974 vintage 9mm Beretta from under the seat. With a ten shot clip, it was a honey of a gun. There weren't many of these manufactured yet. He attached a silencer to it and slid it into his inside coat pocket and went back into the apartment. The men were all still seated at the table, making Ben's job a little easier. Ben emerged into the room with his right hand inside his coat, making it bulge out and his left arm around the bulge as if holding something. Charlie looked up first. "Hey, where's that . . . ?" Before Charlie could finish the sentence, Ben drew out the gun and put a round into Charlie's forehead, then fired rapidly at the others. Giani was too slow to react and took his while still seated. Fred was halfway to a standing position when a bullet put him down. Tom Jacobs was the only one quick enough to make it out of his chair. His back was toward Ben so he tried to dodge him to his right, but there was nowhere to go. Ben sent a bullet into the back of Tom's skull.

Ben checked to see that all were dead. Once satisfied, he went into the kitchen and grabbed a plastic garbage bag from under the sink. He dropped his gun into the bag and left the apartment. When he got to his car, he put his gloves and overcoat in the bag. Then he reached under the driver's seat and took out two bricks. They also went into the bag. He slid into the driver's seat and put the bag on the passenger side floorboard. He drove to the highway and headed north over the Mystic River Bridge. When he was halfway over the bridge with no other cars in sight, he stopped his car, quickly got out and sent the bag over the railing into the river. Ben took a deep breath as he got back into his car and drove home.

Chapter Four

Maria awoke with a start as she heard a car's horn blast outside her apartment. The sound of the engine faded as it drove away. Just the sound of Sunday morning traffic. She sat up on the edge of the bed, yawned and stretched and then made it to her feet. The morning fall air felt cool against her skin.

After Maria had showered, dressed and straightened up the apartment, she headed out the door of her brownstone wearing baggy jeans, tennis shoes and a black turtleneck sweater. She wore a waist length brown jacket to take the chill off. She stepped onto the wide sidewalk and headed two blocks east to the coffee shop she liked.

It was a below sidewalk level place with a few tables outside. Maria went inside. She went up to the counter, got in line behind a couple and reached inside her purse. As the people in front of her gave their orders and moved away, the owner spoke to her.

"What'll it be?" he asked, smiling.

"Large decaf, please, with cream and sugar."

"Anything else?"

"I'll have a blueberry bagel with plain cream cheese, thanks." She held a five dollar bill in her hand as she looked up at the television on a shelf in the corner behind the counter. The morning news was playing on a local Boston station.

"Here ya go," said the owner.

Maria paid the man, gathered her coffee and bagel and moved to a small table near the front of the shop. She sat with her back to the wall and angled herself so she could see the doorway entrance on one side and the television at the other end. Two more women came in. A soap commercial ran on the TV.

"Welcome to your mid-morning news on WBOS-TV. I'm Bill Chase reporting," the voice from the television announced. "An apparent Mob-related massacre took place early this morning in the North End. An anonymous phone call led police to a private apartment where four men were found shot to death gangland style, while they were playing poker."

Maria looked up at the TV and put down her coffee cup. She listened for more information. As the anchorman spoke, the camera showed the front of the townhouse where the killings took place.

"One of the victims has been identified as Tom Jacobs, a respected reporter for the Boston Tribune. He was known to mingle with underworld figures as a means of obtaining information for stories he covered. Tom was with the Tribune for over six years. He lived alone in Cambridge."

Ben occasionally played poker in late night games with business friends, thought Maria as a chill ran through her. She took a sip from her coffee.

The anchorman continued.

"Other victims have been identified as Charles *The Senator* Senatori, Fred *Freddy* Di Nardi, and Giani Bertoli. All but Bertoli had criminal records. They were all known figures to the Boston Police Department."

The names meant nothing to her. She went back to her coffee. When finished, Maria left a tip on the table, put on her jacket and left the coffee shop. She walked quickly back to her apartment. She was concerned that Ben hadn't come back last night as he had promised, but she thought it best not to call him. He didn't like it if she pried into his affairs. He only wanted her to know what he told her, when he told her.

She turned the key to her apartment door with one hand, and the knob with the other. She stepped inside and dropped her purse and jacket on a nearby chair. Her eyes opened wide when she heard the sound of the toilet flush from the bathroom.

"Hi, Baby," said Ben, as he came into the living room.

He walked up to her and took her in his arms, running his hands down her back as far as he could reach and back up again. Holding on to her sides, he pushed back slightly to look at her face.

"Are you okay?" he asked.

"I'm . . . fine," she said slowly. "I was just. . . . I'm just glad to see you. I thought you were coming back last night."

Ben shrugged. "I said I'd be back later. This is later."

Maria nodded without looking directly at Ben.

"You know, Maria, you're way overdressed compared to the last time I saw you. Get the idea?"

"Yeah, I get it," she said, forcing a smile.

Ben walked to the bedroom and stood at the door, waiting for Maria to enter. As she went in, Ben spoke to her, his tone now serious.

"There's a favor I need from you, Baby."

"Okay," she answered.

"In case anybody asks, I was here all night with you, okay?"

Maria looked at Ben as if she'd just been given marching orders instead of being asked a favor.

"Okay," she said, nodding.

She turned her head toward Ben and opened her mouth as if she were about to ask him something, but then thought the better of it. She looked back at the floor and nodded.

About an hour later, Maria awoke and found Ben getting dressed. "Thanks for . . . everything, kid. Fantastic, as usual. Like you said last night, I'm Mr. Hit and Run. Business calls."

Maria got dressed and spent a few hours doing some schoolwork, focusing on a poem she was writing for her Creative Writing class.

Maria liked being in college. She was both happy and sad to be in her senior year at New Sussex College. The college life in a small New Hampshire community offered a stark contrast to her life in Boston. The college experience brought her into contact with kids a couple of years younger who were just about to start their adult lives and careers. They were full of tomorrows. Her Boston life was full of men Ben's age: thirty-ish and older; men of authority, power and wealth. And risk.

Seven o'clock came quickly for Maria. Her date for the Boston Pops performance would be here soon. She selected a tight-fitting dark green dress with a hemline at the knee and a low curved neckline that was bound to get some smiles from the gray-haired businessman she would meet tonight.

The buzzer in Maria's apartment sounded, signaling the arrival of her customer for the evening. She pressed the button to speak.

"Hello," she said.

"Hello. Is this Maria?" a voice asked.

"Yes it is."

"This is Wayne Sullivan, your date tonight."

"I'll be right down," said Maria. She put on her cream-colored coat and scarf, grabbed her black purse and headed to meet her evening.

A silver-haired man in a dark suit and grey overcoat met her at the front of her building. She saw a black limo double-parked in front of them.

"Hello, Mr. Sullivan. I'm Maria," she said as she offered a hand. The man grasped it softly in both of his hands.

"Please," he said smiling, "call me Wayne."

Maria had left her coat unbuttoned enough to show off her revealing neckline. Wayne noticed. Now, as Maria slid into the limo her dress rose up a few inches on her legs and she let her coat fall to give her maximum exposure. Wayne smiled and slid into the backseat beside her.

"I hope you like swing jazz," he said to Maria. "The Pops is doing a tribute to Duke Ellington and others from the big bands of the forties."

"Oh, I do," answered Maria. "Sometimes I wish I were born earlier so that I could have heard them in person. I have a small collection of big band recordings. I especially like Sinatra when he was very young and starting out with Tommy Dorsey."

"That's wonderful, my dear. Then we should have a great evening."

He smiled and gently patted Maria's exposed thigh, leaving his hand there. *At least the music will be good,* she thought to herself. *And the money.*

The concert didn't disappoint Maria. When it was over, the couple got back in the limo and returned to the Back Bay, pulling up to a large townhouse on Commonwealth Avenue. Maria held on to Wayne's arm as they approached the door. A doorman opened the elegant front door and nodded at Wayne. Maria gazed about the large, circular foyer as Wayne took her coat and handed it, along with his own, to a young woman in the coat check room.

"A private club," said Wayne, anticipating Maria's question. "Rather nice, don't you think?"

"Very," she replied.

He escorted her through the hallway lined with elegantly framed paintings and entered a dining room where they were seated at a table for two. Several other people were also in the room having dinner and cocktails.

They enjoyed an excellent meal. Maria had Atlantic Salmon with rice pilaf, a garden salad and a glass of Pinot Grigio. Wayne chose prime rib with baked potato, string beans and a Merlot. They followed it with a light desert.

"This is a beautiful old building, Wayne. How long have you been a member of this club?"

"Oh, quite a while, dear. It's very exclusive. Only successful men such as myself can qualify."

A tall, thin man in a dark blue pinstriped suit came by the table.

"Hello, Wayne," he said. "I hope you are having an enjoyable time. It's always good to see you when you're in town."

"The evening couldn't be better. Let me introduce you to Maria."

"Hello, Maria, welcome to our club. My name is Sid Green."

"Nice to meet you," said Maria.

"I hope to see you here again," said Sid. He nodded at Wayne as if sending a signal, handed him a small envelope and then left.

Wayne stood up from the table and gestured to Maria. "Come, my dear. Let me show you another part of the club."

He escorted Maria out of the dining room. He led her toward the back of the townhouse to an exposed elevator. They ascended to the third floor, got out and walked across the hall. Taking the envelope out of his pocket and extracting a key from it, Wayne opened the door. Maria entered into a spacious room with an oriental rug, several large paintings and a king sized, canopy bed. Wayne walked over to a well stocked bar and asked Maria if she wanted a drink.

"Scotch, neat," she replied.

The limo, the concert and the dinner were all foreplay. Now it was time for her to earn her money.

Chapter Five

After leaving Maria's on Sunday morning, Ben Secani drove back to his house in the Orient Heights section of East Boston, where he lived alone in a second story, two bedroom flat in a white clapboard building with a small yard. On the way, he stopped at a pay phone on a corner and made a call. When a voice answered, Ben simply said, "It's done." He got back into his car and continued home. He pulled into the driveway and parked his T-Bird in the detached garage, feeling satisfied.

The assignment had come from his immediate boss in Boston, but it originated in Providence. Ben would never be told the name of the guy, but he didn't have to be told. It had to be Link, called that because of his tie to the New York crime families. He was the Boss of all Bosses in New England and ran all the businesses east of the Connecticut River.

Link didn't care for the drug business. He'd been a young man during Prohibition, when he'd begun his rise in the Mob. Making, selling and drinking booze were manly things, a good business to be in, and the Volsted Act only made it better. When narcotics crept into the business, Link hated it—but the profits helped him enlarge his empire, finance new ventures, take care of his enemies and enjoy the good life. The drug culture of the Sixties was centered on a bunch of counter-culture freaks. If some dumb long-haired jerk wanted to get high at a rock concert in some cow pasture and died of an overdose, the hell with him.

Young kids were another matter. Link didn't want drugs going to high school kids, or worse yet, even younger ones. But that was what was happening, and Link wanted to stop it. He'd heard that Fred Di Nardi was selling out of his Boston club to teenagers. "The hell with Providence," Fred once said to warnings that his business was frowned on. "This is my club and I do whatever I want in here. The money's good and green, isn't it!"

Ben picked the date and time for the hit. Only his immediate boss, Joe Vito, knew Ben was the trigger man. The fewer people who knew what was going on, the better.

The rush of confidence quickly faded as fatigue caught up with Ben. He dropped his coat on a chair as he walked into the bedroom, kicked off his shoes and flopped on the bed. Sleep came easily.

A few hours later, Ben awoke. He checked his watch. Grabbing his wallet and gun, he put on his coat and moved quickly down the stairs of his building, exiting through the front door. He hopped into his T-Bird and drove downtown to the Prudential Center and parked in the underground garage, one level down. Ben hiked the stairs up to the main, open air level below the Pru tower. He looked around carefully and paced slowly back and forth. Finally, he saw someone in a long top coat moving his way.

The approaching figure stopped a few feet away and sat on an iron bench. Ben moved to the bench and took a seat beside the thin, young man.

"Ben, how are ya?" the man said.

"Just fine, Jimmy, but more to the point, how have you been this week?"

"I've been happy this week," said Jimmy *Slick* Morelli. "And you're gonna be happy, too."

They spoke while looking straight ahead, not making eye contact with each other. Jimmy took a brown bag out of his coat pocket and put it between them. He reached inside and drew out a sandwich wrapped in paper. He held it with both hands and motioned with his head to Ben. "Care for a sandwich? Go ahead. You'll like it."

Ben reached into the bag and slowly pulled out something wrapped in the same type of paper. Ben didn't look at it, slipping it in his inside coat pocket.

"A couple large ones," said Jimmy.

Jimmy Morelli was in his late twenties and had been working for Ben for over a year. He was responsible for providing *protection insurance* for some merchants in various parts of town, but mostly in South Boston. It was collection day for Ben. He'd set the date, time and location

Connections   Steven P. Marini

two or three days in advance and Jimmy would pay Ben his share.

"I had some good luck with a few chumps at the bus terminal this week," said Slick. "So there's a little extra."

"Nice going."

Medium height and thin muscled, Jimmy could handle himself in a fight, but he preferred to use his wits. One of his tricks was to *shortchange* suckers out of a few bucks. Jimmy would ask a stranger to make change for a large bill in exchange for several smaller ones, supposedly of the same amount. He'd mix up the exchange. and the sucker would find himself in a fast-talking *clarification* with Slick Jimmy, who made off with a few bucks more than he had to begin with. By the time the confused mark figured it out, Jimmy would have disappeared into a crowd. He was getting so good he could pick up a hundred extra in a given day. Of course, he couldn't work the same spot every time, so he only did this a few days a week, moving around town with the scam.

"This is nice, Jimmy. Only trouble is you're working in too small a territory. I want you to expand. Go out into the suburbs around Route 128, say about six o'clock. Hit the train stations where the wholesome businessmen will be arriving after a hard day at the office. Try that a few times and let's see how it works."

"Okay, Ben. I'll give that a shot. Anything you say. Hey, ah, Ben," Jimmy spoke haltingly, not sure if he should continue. Then he summoned up some courage and spoke again. "You know that chick you got working out of the Back Bay. I got a look at her when you had me drive you around. She's pretty fine stuff. Any chance I could get a freebie sometime?"

Ben stared at Jimmy without answering. Then he stood up and walked over to the wall that looked out over Boylston Street. He turned back to Jimmy Slick and motioned him to come over. When Jimmy got beside him, Ben put his left hand on Jimmy's shoulder and drew him a little closer.

"Jimmy," he said. "I gotta tell ya . . ."

Jimmy waited for the rest of the sentence but instead of words, he got a right hand blow to the midsection.

Jimmy started to buckle forward but Ben held him up, in case someone noticed.

"Don't even think about her!" demanded Ben. "Do you understand?" Jimmy nodded, still unable to talk. "She's out of your league, way out." Ben still held onto Slick. "Don't ever ask me that again."

"I didn't mean anything, Ben, really," said Jimmy, catching his breath and still grimacing from the blow. "Yeah. Okay. I understand."

"Good," said Ben, as he turned toward Jimmy and straightened his coat. "It's good we can talk these things out. I'll see you again in two weeks. I'll get in touch. And that bonus you brought me, let's make that a habit."

Jimmy looked at Ben, his mouth open as he realized that this had been a bad idea of his. "Yeah, sure."

Ben nodded with satisfaction at the result of this exchange and headed for the stairs leading down to the garage. Jimmy thrust his hands into his coat pockets and stomped one foot on the ground. Ben smiled as he walked away. It's always best to keep a good thing in your own yard.

Later that day, Ben drove downtown to Club 77 on Washington Street. A well built go-go dancer was just finishing her number on the platform in the center of the club above the dance floor. Ben went up to the bar and ordered a beer from Big Ted, the bartender, who stood about six foot, ten inches, and at age fifty-one, had filled out his once very thin frame.

"Hi, Ben, how ya doing?" asked Ted.

"Good, Ted, good."

The club had only a handful of patrons at that hour of the day. Ben sipped his beer. Ted waited to see if Ben would say anything else, but he was quiet. The go-go dancer climbed down the ladder from her platform and picked up a towel off one of the rungs. She wiped herself off, then draped it around her neck with the ends just covering her bare breasts and headed over to the bar. Ben motioned with his finger to join him. The small woman walked up to Ben and playfully nudged him with her hip like a hockey player delivering a hip check.

"Hi, Ben. What's up?" she asked, gazing into Ben's eyes.

"Get the young lady a drink, Ted," ordered Ben.

"A cold one, Ted, thanks," she said, smiling at Ben.

"Ginny, I need you to do me a favor," said Ben, smiling back at the dancer.

"For you, Ben, just name it."

Ben drew a pen out of his shirt pocket and grabbed a napkin and started to write. "When you're off duty, give this guy a call." He slid the napkin with Jimmy Morelli's phone number on it across the bar to Ginny. Her face showed disappointment.

"Who's this, a relative?"

"Now, now. I want you to be nice to him. He's a business associate and he could use a pick-me-up." Ben took some cash out of his pants pocket, rolled it and slipped it into Ginny's G-string. Ginny had been around the block several times over and knew better than to resist. Ben could be very persuasive.

Ginny grabbed her beer, nodded at Ben and started to walk away to the dressing room behind the bar. It was not welcomed this time when she felt Ben's hand slap her ass.

Ben watched Ginny walk away while he took another drink.

"Is he in?" he asked Ted.

Ted nodded and Ben put down his empty glass and headed for the same doorway as Ginny. He went through it and walked past the room that Ginny entered. He reached a closed door a few steps away. Ben knocked. "Come in."

Joe Vito was seated at a desk facing the door. Medium height but very powerfully built, Joe had climbed the ranks in the organization, making his mark as a very reliable hit man. He was especially adept with a knife. They were easy to clean up and dispose of and they left nothing for the ballistics lab. As his reputation grew as a hit man, he also became quite effective as a collector and persuader. When people who owed money saw Joe Vito paying them a visit, they always managed to come up with the cash to make their payment.

Joe loved the Combat Zone and all the businesses there. As he moved up in the organization, he also acquired ownership of a couple of those establishments. Club 77, or The Club, as it was called, became his home base for gambling, prostitution, loan sharking, and protection, his main enterprises. Joe had brains, too, and as Boston politicians ranted more frequently about cleaning up the Zone, he started acquiring more properties that he'd sell at a high profit when and if the time Zone fell to urban redevelopment.

The two men looked at each other, but dispensed with any greetings. Ben sat in a chair facing the desk.

"So, everything went okay," said Joe.

"Yeah. Too bad there was a crowd in the house, but I couldn't leave any witnesses, especially that reporter. Nobody's gonna miss him. Bertoli, too. He was small time. It'll give the press something to write about for a while. As for Charlie, that's too bad but it couldn't be helped, I guess."

Joe looked at Ben, leaning forward in his chair. "You didn't know this, but Charlie was part of the job."

"What? How was that?"

Joe took a bottle out of the desk drawer along with two glasses. He poured a shot of whiskey for himself and motioned to Ben. Ben waved him off. Joe gulped down the booze and put the glass down.

"Charlie was working on a new nickname," said Joe. "He was gonna change from *The Senator* to *The Rat*. He's been talking to the METS."

The Metropolitan District Commission cops were the oldest uniformed state law enforcement agency in the Commonwealth. They had jurisdiction over all MDC controlled properties and roadways. In addition to uniformed officers, the Metro Police also had a detective unit. They investigated crimes on MDC properties and also provided help, including undercover work, to other communities, the Drug Enforcement Agency and the Federal Bureau of Investigation.

"Geez, I can't believe it."

"Believe it. He was feeding information to that big cop, Contino, in Somerville.

Di Nardi alone wasn't worth the trouble," explained Joe. "But Providence really wanted The Senator. This way, they get two birds with one stone and it confuses the cops about what really happened."

"Yeah, makes sense. So what happens to Di Nardi's place?"

"I get it as my compensation for taking care of things. You get ten per cent of the business, Ben. You did a good job."

"I'll take that shot now."

"I'd throw a big party to celebrate," said Joe. "But we don't want to draw attention to ourselves. It might look too suspicious. But there's nothing wrong with having a small celebration right here." Ben smiled as Joe got up from his desk and walked over to the office door. "Let me see who's in the dressing room."

"Ah, just so that you know, not Ginny. I sent her on a mission of mercy for one of my guys."

"Not a problem," said Joe. He walked across the hall into the dressing room and spotted two other dancers. "Ladies, come into my office. Let's conduct some business."

"I'm in the booth in thirty minutes," explained one of the dancers.

Joe rubbed his palms together. He motioned the women into his office with a sweep of his arm. "You'll be back in plenty of time."

Chapter Six

Jack Contino poured himself a mug of coffee and walked with it to the second story window of the MDC police South Boston barracks on Old Colony Street. Gray clouds rolling in from the east were not helping big Jack's mood one bit.

"So, what do you think, Leo?" asked Jack. "Do you believe that Senatori was just in the wrong place at the wrong time?"

"Looks that way to me," said Leo, seated at his desk while shuffling papers and puffing on a cigar. Leo Barbado had worked with Jack since their early days on the force and they had been partners for seven years. This was not a happy time for these veterans of the MDC police.

"What dumb luck, rotten dumb luck!" exclaimed Jack. "We spend—what, five—six months cultivating a snitch and he gets blown away in a hit on somebody else. Can it really be that simple?"

"Hey, a lot of bad guys moved through that apartment of his. Every now and then somebody in the Mob pisses somebody off big time and gets themselves caught in some other guy's crosshairs. Somebody in Charlie's position, you know, not too big-time; entertains a lot of guys at his place, could get in the line of somebody's fire. It's been known to happen."

"Yeah, just the kind of guy who could be valuable to us, but not too essential to them. So who do you figure the hit was on, Di Nardi?"

"That would be my guess. Bertoli was an old guy past his prime. He was never a big player, and he liked to spread money around the Zone. The reporter, he was harmless. They just used him to their advantage. Why hit either of them? Word had it that Di Nardi was out of favor with the Rhode Island boys."

Jack sipped his coffee and looked at Leo. "Enough to get taken out?"

"I guess so." The two MET cops sipped, puffed, shrugged and paced while they tried to figure out the recent gangland massacre.

The barracks room was big enough for eight detectives' desks and a uniformed receptionist, who greeted people as they came through the double door entrance.

"Looks like you two have your work cut out," said one of the other detectives from across the room.

"With a quadruple hit, I think there'll be enough work for all of us," said Jack. "So don't make any dinner plans tonight."

The phone at the receptionist's desk rang and the young woman officer answered it. "Call for you, Jack, line two."

Jack slid into his chair, pushed a button on his phone and picked up the receiver. "Detective Contino here. Hello, Agent Nelson." Jack threw a glance over at Leo. "Nice to hear from you. How was your weekend?"

"Tell us what happened, Jack," said the caller. "We don't like this. We had high hopes for this snitch."

"So did we. Look, this caught us off-guard, too. We never saw it coming. Two of these guys are small potatoes, one may be in the dog house with somebody and one of them is our boy. At first glance, it looks like he may have just been collateral, like the other two."

"Well, you're going to have to take another look and make it a deep one."

"You got any specific suggestions?"

"Just keep a sharp eye out before you make a move. Give it time to see how it plays. See if anybody significant leaves town or if there's any major business. Somebody stands to benefit from this hit, a payoff of some kind. See if you can catch it. And bring Agent Watson up to speed. She'll need to know what's going on."

"I thought she was working on another assignment. We can handle this without her."

"Look, I'm not assigning her to this case, but just keep her informed, that's all."

"Okay, Agent, will do. We'll be in touch, no doubt."

Jack was surprised the FBI hadn't called even earlier. Heck, it was almost nine o'clock in the morning. Jack repeated the Agent's instructions to Leo and then he finished his coffee, ready to dig into things.

Jack was right about there being plenty of work for the other detectives. Three others were already back at the crime scene. The lab people had completed their work. Fingerprints were dusted off playing cards, glasses, bottles and door knobs. Blood samples were collected. Bullet holes were looked for but not found. The detectives canvassed the neighborhood for possible witnesses. As could be expected, none showed up. Nobody heard anything. Nobody saw anything.

Jack Contino and Leo Barbado had their own special approach to this case. They needed to find out who did it, but they also needed to know why. They'd been developing Charlie Senatori to snare as many fish as possible from the New England underworld. In return, they'd keep him out of that mess in Connecticut.

The New England was run from Providence and controlled the two major subsets in Boston; the North End and the Winter Hill in Somerville. Providence was, in turn, run by New York. Boston's boss, Edward *Fat Eddie* Grosso, reported to the boss of all New England bosses, Arnold *The Link* Ciccante in Providence. The FBI knew the pecking order but had never been able to connect any of the major players to crimes big enough for long prison terms. They'd sent Agent Watson to the Boston office to help look for such connections.

Leo swung around in his chair and looked at Jack, puzzled. "So what do we do now? If Nelson wants us to sit tight, we could fly down to Miami for a few days and catch some sun."

"Not likely," said Jack. "I've had the victims' personal belongings sent over. Let's go down and check them out."

They took the elevator to the basement level, exited and crossed the hall to enter a door with smoked glass but no signage. They entered through the door and came to a check-in desk.

"Detective Contino," said Jack, identifying himself to the uniformed officer on the other side.

"And Detective Barbado, I presume," said the uniform. "Just sign in, fellas, and then follow me."

The two detectives did as instructed and followed the officer into the hallway to another room three doors down. It was small, with chairs around a table holding four wire baskets containing the murder victim's personal effects.

Looking around at the bare, cinder block walls, Leo commented, "I love what you've done with the place."

"Take your pick," said Jack. Leo moved to the side of the table across from Jack and grabbed the two nearest baskets. There were name tags tied to each one.

"Looks like I've got Jacobs and Bertoli," announced Leo. They put each basket on a separate table to make sure they didn't mix up any items. Jack began pulling items out of the first basket he took hold of, the one with the name Senatori on it.

"Why does that not surprise me?" asked Leo. Jack just grinned and continued his search. There was nothing of great significance in Charlie's basket: a watch, a large brass belt buckle, some cigars, a wad of cash and a wedding ring.

Leo had similar luck with Bertoli's basket and moved on to the one with Tom Jacob's belongings. He found a billfold and looked through it, pulling a couple of credit cards, a driver's license, a union card, and some cash: the usual stuff. After putting the billfold down, he grabbed at a slim, shirt pocket-sized notebook, flipped it open and scanned through the pages to the last entry. Last Saturday's date appeared at the top, Oct. 20th.

"What's that?" asked Jack, eyeballing Leo's find.

"The reporter had a little notebook. His last entry was Saturday. It says poker night at Senatori's place, expect Charlie, Bertoli, Di Nardi, maybe Secani. Who's Secani?"

"Don't know. Let me see that."

Jack took the notebook and read the last entry again, then flipped through the previous entries. He read through several pages and took out a small notebook of his own, writing in it the name Secani. "He's new to me. Let's check on Secani through the NCIC."

Jack and Leo completed their examination of the baskets and went back to the check-in desk. They signed out and took the elevator to the ground level floor.

"Leo, why don't you go over to that liquor warehouse that Bertoli ran and talk to the people there. Find out whatever you can. I'm going over to the Tribune." The detectives headed to separate cars and drove off.

It was a short drive down the boulevard to the Boston Tribune, the largest newspaper in Boston. Jack had a hunch the newspaper management might be sitting on a lead or two. He pulled up to the security gate at the entrance and flashed his badge at the guard.

"Detective Jack Contino, MDC Police," said Jack to the heavyset, aging guard at the gate. *Looks like a retiree in his next life,* thought Jack to himself. *Probably an ex-MET.*

"Good morning, Detective," greeted the guard. He pulled a parking pass from a stack that he held in his hand, along with a clipboard, and gave it to Jack, who placed it on his dashboard. "Follow the signs to the visitors section, right that way," he said, pointing. The guard wrote Jack's name on the clipboard and recorded his plate number as Jack drove into the lot.

Once inside the lobby of the massive, sprawling building, Jack identified himself to one of two receptionists at the main desk. "I need to speak with your managing editor, now."

The receptionist got the point. She figured there would be police in the building today. "Yes, Sir," she said and then moved quickly back to a desk with a phone system control center on it. She pressed two buttons, waited a second and then said, "There's a Detective Contino from the MDC Police here to see Mr. Higgins." She pressed another button ending the call and walked back to Jack. "It'll be just a minute," she said. Jack nodded and paced a small area as he hoped for a productive visit.

Jack looked at a bank of three elevators in the lobby. After a short wait, one of the elevator doors opened and out stepped a man of medium height and trim build in an expensive-looking dark, three-piece suit. He appeared to be about forty years old, handsome, gray slightly infiltrating the hair at his temples. He looked younger than Jack expected.

"Detective Contino?" he asked, extending a hand. Jack acknowledged him and returned the hand shake.

33

"Let's go up to the office, shall we?" He motioned toward the elevators. Jack was a cop, an old cop, and he looked like it. This guy didn't fit the mold of a newspaper man. He didn't look like Perry White to Jack.

Once in the elevator, the man pushed a button for the fifth and top floor of the building. "I appreciate your taking time to see me without me calling ahead. I'm sure you're very busy today, Mr. Higgins," said Jack. The man was looking at the floor but raised his head to speak.

"Actually Detective, I'm not Mr. Higgins. I'm his secretary."

The elevator reached the top floor, and the men walked out into a large hallway with a high ceiling and polished cherry wood paneling on the walls. They passed several doors, all with high arches over them, and came to one at the end of the hall. Jack moved toward it. "Ah, that's the publisher's suite," said the secretary. "Right this way."

They entered a beautifully furnished outer office with a door to an inner sanctum at the back. That door opened and an older looking man with a full head of gray hair walked through it and went right up to Jack.

"Chuck Higgins. Nice to meet you," he said, shaking Jack's hand firmly. His long sleeve white shirt was a bit wrinkled and his tie was loosened in front of an opened collar. Okay, this wasn't Perry White, either.

They went into Mr. Higgins's office. Higgins took a seat in a comfortable looking leather chair and motioned Jack toward an identical one beside it, separated only by a corner table.

"I understand you're with the MDC Police," said Higgins. Jack nodded. "And you're here about Tom Jacob's murder?" queried Higgins. Jack nodded again. "Well, I'm anxious to help in any way I can," said Higgins. "We're prepared to put the full resources of this newspaper to work, if you need us. I can't tell you what a shock this is to the entire Tribune. Tom was an excellent reporter and very well liked here. Do you have any leads so far, Detective?" asked Higgins, sitting forward in his chair.

"It's very early in the investigation, Mr. Higgins," said Jack.

"Please, call me Chuck."

Again, Jack nodded. Like a good reporter, Higgins took the initiative once again. "How is it that the MDC Police are involved?" After twenty-five years at the Tribune, he knew full well what roles the MDC Police played in Boston law enforcement, but wanted to hear Jack's answer, looking for anything that would help satisfy his own curiosity.

"Good law enforcement is a cooperative effort in a big city. Sometimes we have to pitch in with other organizations; city, state, even feds sometimes."

"I see."

Before Higgins could ask another question, Jack leaned forward, beating him to the punch. "Chuck, how often did Jacobs play in these late night card games?"

"I'm not sure. It was his job to mix with the people, so he took advantage of every opportunity he could."

"How long had he been covering the Mob?"

"Over two years now. He gained their confidence. They liked him and enjoyed seeing his stories with fake names substituted for themselves. It was like a game to them."

"Was he working on a hot story, something that might make the guys nervous?"

"He was always looking for something big, but he wasn't out to play cop. He tried to capture their everyday life. His stories were meant to show what it was like living in the Mob."

"I've been a cop for a long time and I know you have to be protective about the newspaper's sources, but it doesn't take a genius to figure out that the other guys at that poker game were among Jacob's contacts. Are there others we need to know about?"

Higgins turned his head to one side, signaling that Jack was treading on thin ice. "If I start mentioning names, some guys will head for the hills and our well of sources will dry up."

"Okay. But if I name somebody, can you at least tell me if it means anything to you?"

"Fair enough."

Jack took a small piece of paper out of his pocket and read out loud, "Secani; S-e-c-a-n-i. Last name, I guess. Don't know the first."

Higgins looked down for a second, then shook his head sideways. "No, that doesn't ring any bells, not at all."

Jack let out a sigh of disappointment and crumpled the paper in his hand. There was a long silence and then Jack started to get out of the chair. He reached into his coat pocket and took out a business card, handing it to Higgins. "Thanks, Chuck. I know this is a hard time for you and your folks. Sometimes, we lose one of our own, too."

"I know you do. Thanks."

*****

Leo Barbado went to the liquor distributorship, South Shore Beverage, located along Hancock Avenue in Quincy. The business was up and running full steam, as if the plant's General Manager hadn't just been gunned down a couple of days earlier. Leo met a man named Frank Damone who'd been an assistant to Giani Bertoli and was apparently running the plant, like a baton had been directly passed to him without question.

What Leo didn't know was that Damone had been groomed by Giani to take over. Bertoli's skimming small amounts from the business was no secret to Frank. Bertoli had promised to teach him how one day. In the meantime, Bertoli paid Damone occasional bonuses to keep him happy and quiet, building a layer of insulation for himself.

"So, you don't know any of these other people who were at the poker game with Bertoli?" asked Leo, sitting in Damone's office just off the warehouse floor. The buzzing sound of forklifts moving to and from the stacks of pallets holding liquor cases was like an undercurrent as the two men talked.

"I know the guy liked to spend his money up at the Combat Zone and he played the ponies a lot, but he never mentioned anybody by name that I can recall. He kept pretty much to himself around here. But the word had it that he ran with some rough guys in his younger days."

"Yeah. We heard that, too."

Although Giani Bertoli had a clean record, he'd often been seen by the police in the company of some known thugs and racketeers over the years. He made good money from his skimming at South Shore Beverage and spread it around. He even made some investments in real estate that paid off well, adding to his income stream. He stayed clear of any specific involvement with the Mobsters that could get him in trouble and end his comfortable position. His money was a welcomed sight at poker games.

Leo looked toward the warehouse, nodding in the direction of the office door with his head. "Don't you guys observe a day of mourning for the guy?"

"Well, no disrespect to the dead, but we've got customers to serve. Besides, the funeral date hasn't been announced. Some of us will make it to that. Hey, I liked the guy."

Perhaps it was a luckless day, or maybe it was just too soon for any useful information to reach the surface. It all stayed below the surface. Perhaps the days ahead would be more productive. Watch for any significant activity, as Agent Nelson had advised. Leo got up and handed Damone a card as he made his exit. "Give me a call if you hear anything interesting."

After Leo left, Damone sat comfortably in what had been Bertoli's chair, a smile on his face. Giani had been sitting on a gold mine, and now Frank was watching the sluice.

Chapter Seven

Maria hated getting up early on Monday mornings and making the drive back to New Hampshire to make her nine o'clock class. *The cost of doing business in the big city,* she thought to herself. But she'd be making a nice bank deposit this afternoon, thanks to Mr. Wayne Sullivan. She'd be able to keep a healthy amount out for herself.

Maria pulled into the parking lot of the Danson Building, the center of this small college campus, and parked her blue Volkswagen Squareback. She had made good time on the highway and had about thirty minutes until class started. She grabbed her book bag and went into the Student Union food court for a cup of coffee. As she took her cup in hand, Maria noticed Sue Fox seated at a corner table with an open notebook in front of her and a cup of hot tea. She walked over to the table and took a seat across from Sue, dropping her bag on the floor bedside her chair.

"Hey, Suzie Q, how was your weekend?" asked Maria as she sat down.

Sue looked up from her notebook and sighed. "It's a shame you always have to work on weekends. You miss out on so much here."

"Oh, some big doings for Sue this weekend?"

"No, not so much, it's just that you miss the campus experience in general, and it's our senior year."

"Did it ever occur to you that maybe I gain some things in Boston that you guys don't have?"

"Like what, specifically?"

"Oh, you know, the city experience in general."

They both laughed.

"Well, whatever you do for work down there, you seem to like it."

Maria gave a nod. "Like I've said, it's just some office work—dull stuff, for a kind of family business . . . some people who knew my dad. They've been good to me. I've got to pay my own way and try to have something left over when I'm done with school. Then, we'll see," she sighed.

"Well, I just don't want you to grow old before you get some excitement in your life."

Maria and Sue were in a U.S. History class together taught by thirty-one-year-old Martin Douglas, a handsome young instructor who was new to the college that year. Maria was taken by his good looks on the first day of class and selected a seat in the front row. Sue followed Maria's lead and sat right behind her. This class was an elective for Maria, who was a business major.

"You've been reading about the League of Nations," Martin said to his class, his deep voice resonating through the room. "So, what do we know about the League?" he asked to nobody in particular. He broke a lingering silence with another question. "Who started it? Who was the driving force behind it?"

"Woodrow Wilson," answered a ruggedly built young man near the back.

"Wilson was a staunch advocate of the League, but no, he wasn't the one I was thinking of."

"It was a British man," Sue offered to the class. "Edward Grey, the British Foreign Secretary, I believe."

"That's correct. What was its mission?"

Another coed sitting in the middle section said, "It was supposed to prevent war, get countries to disarm and use diplomacy to settle disputes between countries."

"Was it successful?"

There was a slight chuckle to that question from some class members. The Vietnam War was winding down, according to the White House, but was still going on and kids were still being drafted. Maria spoke without raising her hand. "The League is well when sparrows shout, but not so good when eagles fall out."

"Oh. Interesting!" said Mr. Douglas, surprised at the response. "I don't think you read that in your text."

"No. I have a biography of Mussolini. He said it. Of course, he was one of the eagles."

"That's right," said Martin. "Italy, under his leadership, invaded Ethiopia in 1935. He easily defeated the weaker army and committed atrocities against the Ethiopian people in the process. This is probably the most famous of the League's failures."

"Why did he do that?" asked a student.

"He wanted to try to rebuild the Roman Empire around the Mediterranean and North Africa," said Maria, turning her head toward the student.

"Very good, Maria," said Mr. Douglas, smiling warmly at her. Maria was a top student, and Martin Douglas enjoyed having her in his class. She always did her assignments and often seemed to be teaching the other kids, rather than just answering the instructor.

The women headed down the hall to their next classes, Sue to her Ed Psych class and Maria to Economics.

Maria moved toward her seat, but noticed students crowding around a paper taped to the blackboard. One of the boys turned to face the classroom and shouted, "No class today! Cancelled for personal reasons. Yes!"

Maria went up to the board to see for herself. *Okay,* she thought, *here's a chance to get to the bank early.* She walked out to her car and tossed her bag in the passenger front seat, then drove off toward Hillsboro and People's Bank.

At the teller window, a very slender young woman took the deposit slip and cash Maria slipped under the glass partition. She read the amount on the paper and looked at Maria quickly, then turned to her computer terminal and counted out nine one hundred dollar bills. A machine behind the teller buzzed and printed out a receipt. The teller ripped it off the printer, forced a smile and gave Maria the receipt.

Maria left the bank and got back into her car. She made a stop at the state liquor store to pick up some Scotch and vodka. This was followed by a quick trip to the grocery store where she picked up some food, two bottles of wine and a six pack of beer. She put these in the backseat of the Squareback and headed home.

🙞🙞🙞🙞

Later that morning, Martin Douglas was at his office on the second floor of The Inn, the old college administration building that was once a grand country lodging along the old horse and buggy road that connected Concord, Hopkington, Henniker and Hillsboro. Its post and beam construction gave it a lot of character, but some thought it was a fire trap and should be torn down. The fiscal position of the small college prohibited that action, however. It was easier to get Federal dollars and private donations for new construction than renovations. So the old building remained standing and housed the business, registrar, admissions offices, several faculty offices, and the mail room in the musty basement.

Martin prepared his lessons for Wednesday and made notes on each student's work and class participation from today's completed classes. He didn't assign class participation grades per se, but he did record his thoughts if the student participated adequately with a small *A* in the column for that class. If the student had done stand out work, he also marked a plus sign next to the *A*. He used this system to help him make what he called marginal grading decisions, whether to take a student from a *B+* to an *A-*, for instance. Maria had a lot of *A+* marks next to her name on the daily rosters.

Martin was a well respected and popular teacher, only two months into his first semester at New Sussex College. He had left his position at the University of New Hampshire after a tough divorce to teach History and Political Science at NSC, and moved into a two bedroom house just north of town past the *T* intersection of Route 202 and Route 114. It was a white, one-story house with an enclosed front porch on a wooded lot. Set about a quarter of a mile off the main road, it was isolated from neighbors, yet convenient to town. Martin paid an affordable rent and the owner agreed to apply all of it toward the purchase price if Martin offered to buy it after nine months into the twelve month lease. It needed a bit of fix up work, but Martin figured that would be all right over time. The stone fireplace in the living room was the selling point for him, along with the privacy. A detached garage to the right of the house gave shelter to his Jeep Wrangler.

Martin closed his grade book and put it in his briefcase. He decided to spend some time organizing and typing up his research notes on the book project he had begun two years ago on the King Philip War of 1676 in the Plymouth Bay Colony. He had let the work go unattended during the divorce, so now it was a good time to get back to it.

Maria's Squareback moved into Henniker and she slowed down for the blinking overhead light in the center of town. She gave a quick look at her watch. It might be early enough to catch Mr. Douglas in his office. Pulling into the parking lot behind the building, she walked quickly through the back entrance to The Inn, hurried up the back stairway and knocked on the frame of the open office door.

"Excuse me, Mr. Douglas," she said.

Martin looked up from his desk and responded to his unexpected visitor.

"Hello, Maria," he said, pleased to see her. "What can I do for you?" he asked, then realized he sounded like a department store salesman. "I mean . . . come in."

Maria walked slowly into the room and stood in front of Martin's desk.

"Well," she began, "I was driving by and decided to save myself a phone call later. I might have to miss class on Friday. Some personal business has come up that I might have to attend to at home in Boston."

"Oh. Is everything okay?"

Maria paused a moment. "Oh, yeah. It's nothing serious. Well, I work weekends and they said they might need me a little early this Friday. I'll try to get out of it, but I just thought I'd let you know in advance."

"I didn't know you had a job. Don't worry about the class. You're doing just great this semester. You aced the mid-term and are pulling a solid *A* so far, so one class isn't going to hurt you. I know it's none of my business, but are you putting yourself through school, Maria?"

She nodded, both uncomfortable about his inquiry into her personal life and pleased that he seemed to care. "I won't keep you," she said. "I just wanted to let you know about Friday. Thanks. See ya." Maria turned quickly and was gone before Martin could inquire further.

*****

Maria stopped by the corner pharmacy and picked up a copy of the *Boston Tribune* before driving back to the student parking lot at the Danson Building. She got out and walked across the lot, down a short slope and blended into a stream of students heading into the dining hall for lunch. After making her way through the line and selecting a lunch of beef stew and a bottle of Tab, Maria walked carefully over to her usual table, where Sue and her boyfriend Dean were already seated along with three other students. She took a place across from the young couple and put her tray and newspaper on the table.

"Hey, did you hear about that gangland killing in Boston over the weekend?" said Dean "Four guys got it and one of them was a reporter for this newspaper. Man, that sounds like something from back in the days of Elliott Ness, for chrissakes!"

Maria looked up with no expression as she sipped her cola.

"Or out of *The Godfather,*" said Sue. "Get up to date, Dean."

"Yeah, well, whatever. That's really cool, ya know, all that Godfather stuff still can happen. Was it anywhere near your place, Maria?" he asked, leaning on his elbows, as excited as a star struck kid.

"I don't know. Who cares?" she shrugged. "Looks like the Celtics won again last night," she said, glancing at Dean as she slid the sports section out of the paper and nudged it toward him.

"Yeah, I heard the scores on the radio this morning," he said. "Maybe they'll win it all this year."

"What about New York?"

Pleased that Dean had taken the bait, Maria relaxed as Dean spun into a discourse as to why the Knicks were inferior to the Celtics. The stew was hot and the beef tender, just the way Maria liked it.

"And we're gonna beat Keene State tomorrow afternoon," said Dean as he stood up from the table. "I trust you kids will be there to see me in action."

Maria looked up at Sue with a slight smirk on her face.

"We wouldn't miss it," said Sue. Maria gave a slight nod and went back to her lunch.

"Gotta go," said Dean. "I'll leave you two to your girl talk."

He placed his hand on Sue's face, turning her head toward him, kissed her, then picked up his book bag and strutted away.

"Testosterone rush!" declared Maria.

"I'm just glad he plays soccer to burn off some of that," said Sue. The girls chatted until Sue finished her lunch first and went off to her next class. "See you later," said Sue as she walked off. Maria waved.

Taking a sip from her drink, Maria now pulled the newspaper closer and read the story on the lower half of the front page. It was a follow up to the continuing story about the gangland style murders in Boston early Sunday morning. She stared at the paper a bit longer. Could Ben be involved? Why did he want her to lie about his being with her all night?

Chapter Eight

On Thursday night, Martin Douglas didn't feel up to cooking for himself after work, so he decided to go to a local restaurant in Hillsboro, just west of Henniker. Govoni's was the best Italian restaurant around. In fact, it was the only Italian restaurant around, but the food was outstanding, and Martin went there from time to time.

He parked his Jeep in the lot behind the building and walked in through the rear entrance leading to the bar, where he saw Jed Pierce, a friend and fellow faculty member at NSC, seated with a plate of food and a glass of red wine. Martin acknowledged his friend and pulled up a bar stool beside him. "That looks good," he said, eyeing the dish of bowtie pasta with meat sauce that Jed was enjoying.

"It is. Give it a try."

"Actually, I usually have the veal scaloppini."

The bartender asked if he wanted a menu, but Martin declined, ordering the veal with a glass of Chianti. Govoni's was a popular place among the NSC faculty and it was not unusual for colleagues to run into each other there.

"I'm glad you're here, Jed. I've got an issue and maybe you can help me with it."

"Let's see—money, women or liquor? Of course, they all tend to be connected in the long run," he added.

"You know, Jed, you're a fun guy to be around, but sometimes you'd make a perfect stranger."

Martin took a sip from his wine glass. "There's a young woman in one of my American History classes who really intrigues me."

"Oh, Baby! Step away from the coeds!" exclaimed Jed. "That can be real trouble. Beware the teacher-student affair trap."

"No, no. It's not like that. I mean, she really intrigues me. She's different from the other students. I think she's a little older, for one thing, and she doesn't talk or act like the others. I'd really like to get to know more about her, but she's a bit distant."

"Is she good looking?"

"Very."

"Well built?"

"Yeah, I'd say so."

"How long have you been divorced?"

Martin laughed and shrugged his shoulders. "Maybe it is more than just intrigue," conceded Martin. "This is an interesting line of questioning from you, married man. Don't you have a wife and kids at home?"

"Not at the moment, which is why I'm eating here."

"How's that?"

"Pamela is working a second shift at the hospital and the boys have soccer practice, so it's dinner out for old Dad," Jed explained, taking a drink from his wine glass. "Really, Martin, sometimes being on the rebound can lead to unsound decisions."

"It's been over a year since the divorce, and I'm over it. She's off with Mr. Perfect and living happily ever after."

"Mr. Perfect?"

"Yeah. She said she found a guy who was just right for her. He left the academic life to write novels and make good money. No scrambling for tenure at twenty thousand a year. He promised her that they'd travel, meet the beautiful people, spend summers at Martha's Vineyard and never have a care. He was perfect." Martin took a sip of his wine. "You know, she wasn't the woman I thought she was. After five years of marriage, I really didn't know her," Martin's voice trailed off.

Jed's tone changed from friend to advisor. "Seriously, Martin, if you want to get to know this girl better, fine. But you need to be careful. She's not just a coed. She's in your History class."

"She has a friend in the same class named Sue. Maybe I could talk to her," said Martin.

"No, no, no! That's the last direction you want to take. Asking her friend about her? Boy, that would blow your cover!"

The bartender put Martin's dinner down in front of him. A few moments passed silently as the men ate their food and drank their wine. Eventually, Jed's eyes opened wide, as if a light bulb had just lit up.

"Martin, how's that book project of yours coming?"

Martin seemed slightly surprised at the change of subject. "Pretty well. I've done a lot of research and have a ton of notes to arrange and type up, but I hope to begin writing a draft after that. Why do you ask?"

"This might be your opportunity to get . . . familiar with your coed. Why don't you ask her if she'd like a part time job as your assistant on the project? She could help you arrange your notes, get them typed up and that way, she'd be in your office a few hours a week without other students around. It could be temporary, just a few weeks if need be, and you'd have ample opportunity to make some small talk, get to know her a little better." Jed finished talking and sat back on his bar stool, satisfied that he'd shared a pearl of wisdom.

"That's not a bad idea." Martin nodded approvingly and stared at his dinner. "It just might work. I sure hope she's been typing her own papers. I also hope she needs the money. Oh, money! I'd have to pay her, wouldn't I?"

"Ah," shrugged Jed. "Just apply for an extension to your grant." Both men laughed and Martin patted Jed on the shoulder as if to seal a deal.

After dinner, Martin hurried back to his office at NSC, oblivious to the fact that it was after work hours and the big building was quiet. The more he thought about Jed's idea the more he liked it. Martin looked over his collection of boxes with note cards and his file drawers of documents that he'd collected doing his research. He realized that he already had much of the work well organized. That wouldn't do, he thought to himself. He'd have to have more work for an assistant, so he began taking papers out of their files, shuffling them out of any sense of order and piling them up on a shelf. He did the same with his note cards, then mixed them in with his most recent research notes, which really were unorganized and handwritten. He'd have to do some more research to add to the pile. Perhaps a trip to the Wampanoag Museum on Cape Cod soon would be a good idea. He could ask Maria to come along. No, no. It's too soon for that. Don't push your luck. Martin never thought hiring an assistant could be so involved.

"Evening, Mr. Douglas," said a voice, breaking the quiet and Martin's concentration.

The papers he was holding fell out of his hands and spread out on the table. Martin looked like a kid who'd gotten caught with his hand in the cookie jar.

"Hello, Officer Mills," said Martin nervously to Jerry Mills, the campus Security guard making his rounds.

"Everything okay?"

"Yeah, sure. You just startled me, a little, that's all."

Officer Mills looked at the pile of papers then bid good night to Martin. "Just making my rounds." He waved to Martin with his backhand as he walked away. "Don't work too late."

"No, I'm about done here," said Martin, feeling foolish. Maria was making him act like a schoolboy. *Got to stay in professor mode.*

On Friday morning, Martin awoke filled with anticipation. After he showered and shaved, he decided to splash on a little bit of aftershave lotion, something he rarely did. It couldn't hurt, he thought. He picked out a Navy blue blazer to wear over his red turtleneck sweater and gray slacks and then had a light breakfast in his kitchen. Grabbing his black travel bag with his books and papers inside, he jumped in his Jeep and drove to the campus.

Arriving just after eight a.m., Martin went straight to his office, rather than the classroom building. As he approached the back stairway leading up to his floor, he waited for a woman on the way down. "Good morning, Paulette," he greeted her. "Nice day, don't you think?"

Paulette Morrison was a secretary in the Business Office, a petite woman in her late thirties who was always in a pleasant mood. "Certainly is, Martin," she replied, noticing his upbeat tone and manner. She attributed it to being a Friday morning. She looked back at Martin as he passed by, smiled and went into her office.

Martin reminded himself that he had classes to teach and tried vainly to clear his mind of thoughts about Maria. He took some of the research papers out of his bag and then removed some other things to lighten his load. He walked over to the only window in his office and stared out over the lawn in front of The Inn. A few cars passed and several students walked by, wrapped in sweatshirts and fall jackets. He moved to the chair at his desk and began to rehearse how he would make his offer to Maria. *So much for professor mode.*

At eight forty-five a.m., Martin walked over to the Danson Building and scurried into his classroom. He wanted to get there ahead of the students. A few minutes later as they began to trickle into the room, Martin watched for Maria. He saw her friend Sue Fox enter the room with a couple of other girls, but Maria wasn't among them. Then he remembered Maria had told him that she wouldn't be in class today. There was some family issue at home. The thought of not seeing her until Monday left him feeling like he had just taken a cold shower.

Showing grace in the face of adversity is a sign of courage, Martin had heard. He forced himself to get back on track and focus on teaching his class. In the greater scheme of things, this was not great adversity. The weekend would pass and Maria would return to campus. His secret plan would have to wait a few days.

The class hour passed quickly as Martin soon became immersed in his work. He checked attendance, gave some opening remarks and, as always, started a dialogue with the class, asking questions. These were good students and were usually well prepared for class. But Maria was always the most well prepared of them all. He missed her leadership in class this day but was pleased that Sue and some others took up the slack and kept the dialogues lively.

As the students moved out of the room after class, Sue stopped by the instructor's desk and spoke to Martin. "Hi, Mr. Douglas," she greeted him. "Maria told you that she'd be absent today, right?"

"Yeah. Got it covered. I guess there's something at home that needs her attention. Is she okay?"

"Yeah, as far as I can tell. She doesn't talk much about her family life or her weekend job. She just hits the trail every Friday and returns on Monday. It's too bad. I wish she'd stick around once in awhile on weekends for some of the college life, but that's up to her, I guess."

"She works on the weekends?" He recalled Maria mentioning this. Maybe she didn't need the work as a research assistant. Maybe she didn't need the little extra money he could offer her as a research assistant. This was bad news to him.

"Yeah, something in a family business in Boston is about all I know."

Deciding to end this conversation before he showed too much concern for Maria, Martin packed his black bag, thanked Sue for the information, and then left the room. The last hour had been an emotional rollercoaster ride.

Chapter Nine

Jack couldn't help himself. He habitually paced the floor when agitated or angry. Days had passed since the gangland massacre and they still had nothing and another day shift was nearly over. But having a good partner helped. "Jack, I'm just kind of thinking out loud here, so bear with me."

"Okay, pal, I'm open to suggestions, 'cause we're off to a lousy start in this investigation. Get us going."

Leo put his coffee down on the desk in front of him and began to swivel back and forth in his chair. "I used to stop in at Di Nardi's club now and then, you know, continuing professional education."

"Yeah, you're a stickler for staying abreast of your field. Does he still serve Bill's Bourbon, or has he started selling Jack Daniels?"

"Anywho, I recall that Di Nardi had a young lady friend, a real hot number named Nancy Sanders, about mid-twenties and really put together. She hung out at the bar with the customers, like it was a big party every night. Maybe she's heard something. Of course, she's probably in mourning over Fred."

"Like you would be, too, if you just lost your sugar daddy. Let's go pay her a visit."

The ride to Di Nardi's was short, just right for Jack's temperament today. They walked past the tables and went up to the bar. The bartender eyed them carefully.

"Can I help you fellas?"

"You do a pretty good business for late afternoon," said Jack.

"Di Nardi's has a small crowd of regulars this time of day. I think of it as early evening."

Leo was first to show his badge. "Detectives Barbado and Contino and, yeah, you can help us."

"Hey, I sure hope you find his killer quick, but you're not going to find him in here. Why don't you go out and do your job?"

"Maybe part of our job is to call our friends at the IRS and have them come here to check your books," said Jack. "Funny bookkeeping can sometimes lead to a motive for murder."

"I didn't mean anything, guys. I'm just kinda upset about Fred. That's all. So, how can I help?"

"Fred had a girlfriend we need to talk to, name is Nancy Sanders. Is she around?" As soon as Jack spoke Nancy's name the bartender's expression changed.

"No, she's not here."

"Well, how about her address and phone number?"

"I think he had it written down in a book on his desk in case somebody needed to reach him. I'll check."

The bartender disappeared into a back room then reappeared in a minute with the information on a slip of paper.

"Thanks," said Jack. "By the way, who's running this place now that Fred's gone?"

The bartender grabbed a glass and started wiping it. "I just work here. I do what I'm told."

Jack nodded as the detectives turned and walked out.

The unmarked MET car didn't cause a stir in the Hyde Park neighborhood when it pulled up to the curb in front of the old house. Each man surveyed the area as they got out of the car and walked up to the front door. A woman, nice looking, but with some rough times showing on her face, answered the door. The men identified themselves and she let them in, leading them into a small living room, where a young woman, very young, stood in a back doorway. Her short, tight miniskirt showed a mature figure, but her baby face gave her youth away.

"Put your eyes back in their sockets, Detective," said Mrs. Sanders to Leo, who she caught eyeing her daughter. "She's only fourteen."

Leo swallowed and looked down.

"Jodie, let me talk to these men alone, please. Go upstairs for a while, okay?"

Her daughter obeyed without making a sound, but she looked back at the detectives and swayed her way out of the room.

"Mrs. Sanders," said Jack, "we'd like to talk to Nancy. Is she here?"

"Here? Hell, I haven't seen her in a couple of weeks. I thought maybe you had some news for me."

"A couple of weeks? Have you filed a missing persons report?"

She shot a look at Jack that gave him his answer.

Jack looked at Leo and then continued. "Has she ever gone off without telling you where she was going before?"

"Yes, a time or two. Once she was gone over a month. But that was a couple of years ago."

"We know she was friendly with a man named Fred Di Nardi who owned a nightclub in Boston. He was murdered a couple of nights ago."

"I heard about that on the news. Too bad. He was better than most of the guys she's been with. You don't think she's involved with that, like, maybe she was killed, too? Oh God."

"No, Mrs. Sanders." Jack tried to calm her down. "There were four men murdered in an apartment, including Di Nardi. She wasn't there."

"Must be that Sammy White bastard."

Jack and Leo looked at each other quickly.

"No, no," she said. "Not that old ballplayer. This guy is really named Sammy DiFino. Just that he really darkens up in the sun so they call him Sammy White."

Leo looked at Jack and then back at Mrs. Sanders. "We're familiar with that name. Let's just say a lot of police are familiar with that name."

"I'm not surprised. He's a real mean bastard. He started seeing Nancy behind Fred's back. Fred found out about it and they were headed for war. I tried to get Nancy to stop with Sammy White before one of them got killed and she said she was going to end it. It was supposed to be their last date but she didn't come home."

"Did you talk to White about it?" asked Leo.

"Yes, I did. In fact, he came over here two nights later with a friend. He said he loaned Nancy his car and she didn't come back with it. But I don't trust that bastard.

She wasn't a thief. Now he keeps showing up, saying he's hoping she'll be here. But then he hangs around and flirts with Jodie. She likes it. If he touches her, I swear I'll kill him."

"Ah, please don't say things like that to us, Mrs. Sanders," said Jack.

"I'm sorry. But now I'm sure he hurt Nancy. I don't know what to do."

Leo gave Mrs. Sanders his card. "If White comes here and lays a hand on Jodie, call us. She's underage and we'll arrest him for statutory rape. We'll find him and have a talk first to try to prevent him from any more visits here."

"Thank you. Please get to him right away. You know how tempting Jodie can look."

"Don't, ah . . . don't worry, Mrs. Sanders."

As they walked back to their car, Leo spoke. "He was there, at Di Nardi's. We walked right by him at a table."

"Might not be there now. Probably left after our visit."

"From what I know of him, he's not the brightest light in the room. It would be worth checking. Besides, I'm sure we've got an address on him. At least his parole officer does."

They made a swift trip back to Di Nardi's and hurried in. "There he is, same table," said Leo. Sammy (aka Sammy White) DiFino was sitting with two women.

"Please excuse the interruption, but we'd like to talk to you, Mr. DiFino, said Leo.

"Ah, let's see, it's Detective Barbado, I believe."

Jack held up his badge. "And I'm Detective Contino, just to complete the introductions." Jack pulled himself up to his full height.

Sammy White smiled and then looked at the girls. "Scram. These gentlemen seem to need my help." The girls left, and the detectives took their seats.

Jack eyed DiFino for a long moment. They had never met, but Jack knew a bit about the man's reputation as a killer and a henchman for an enemy Jack wanted to put in lock up for a long time, Tommy Shea.

Leo spoke while Jack sat back. "We're actually looking for Fred's girlfriend, Nancy Sanders. Would you happen to know where we can find her?"

"First of all, she's Fred's ex-girlfriend and, second, no. I wouldn't know where she is. Wish I did. She's got my car."

"We heard Nancy had taken up with you. Guess that got under Fred's skin quite a bit, enough to start a battle between you two."

"Now where did you hear that? Actually, Fred was a real stand up guy about it. He knew the best man won. We got along just fine."

"That's not what Nancy's mother told us."

"Well, she's wrong. Say, why were you talking to her?"

"We'll ask the questions, Bucko. We'd like to know where you were the night Fred and the others got killed."

Sammy White smiled and relaxed back in his chair. "So you want to see if I got an alibi. Oh, yeah."

He reached into his sport coat, pulled out pen and paper, then scribbled something down quickly. "There's my alibi. Check it out. All night."

Leo took the paper, read the name on it and slid it to Jack. Their expressions gave Sammy White great satisfaction. It read Tammy Watson. Tammy was an FBI contact who would never win a popularity contest with the MET cops. She was supposed to be helping Jack nail Tommy Shea, but she consistently messed up all traps that they set. She was either stupid, incompetent or something else.

Jack pushed his chair back from the table and stood up, glaring at Sammy White. "We're going to find whoever killed those guys, regardless of Agent Watson. And another thing, stay away from Mrs. Sanders and her teenage daughter. Get it, Sammy? She's underage and if you so much as put a hand on her I'll have you up on statutory rape." Jack and Leo started out.

"How am I supposed to get my car back?"

"Somehow," said Jack over his shoulder, "I don't think you're all that worried about your car. Don't forget our little chat."

Once back in their car, Jack sat shaking his head. "I don't believe that bitch Watson. She's sleeping with the damned enemy."

"Yeah, and he's got a very tight alibi."

"This looks like a dead end for the gang killing."

"What about Nancy Sanders? I'm not buying his story about her and his car."

"Me neither, but until she shows up, one way or the other, there's nothing we can do there. She's got a history of running off and, for all we really know, she could have taken Sammy White's car, regardless of what her mother thinks."

"What about Agent Watson? How do we handle that?"

"I know how I'd like to handle it, if she were a guy. Guess I can't go that way. Maybe I can persuade Agent Nelson to send her back to Washington. Start the car, Leo. Let's get away from this stone wall."

Chapter Ten
1963

In 1963, the Falcone family lived on Dexter Street, just off of Valler Road in East Boston. Maria was thirteen, but was developing like a seventeen-year-old. As her father, Alberto would say, the bees were starting to buzz around her.

One young man who started to notice her was Ben Secani. He lived with his mom, Betty, two doors down from the Falcones. After a two year draft hitch and a tour in Vietnam that introduced him to killing, he returned home a hardened young man. Ben was seven years older than Maria and always saw her as the cute little daughter of his neighbor and friend, Alberto Falcone. In a way, he was a big brother to Maria and kept an eye on her as a favor to Alberto, who'd helped Ben learn about the racing game at nearby Suffolk Downs. Ben's dad had walked out when he was just ten and Alberto often helped the boy by hiring him to do odd jobs, like washing his car and shoveling it out of snow in winter. As he got older, Alberto would take him to the track to watch the horses and eventually to place bets through Alberto.

One spring afternoon, Maria was walking home on her street lined with row houses, followed closely by two older boys who had been hanging around near the school bus stop. They caught up to Maria and flanked her. She hugged her book bag to her chest and kept her eyes forward. The boys began to nudge her and laugh when Maria walked faster.

"Oh Maria, that's one lucky book bag," said one. The other one grinned.

"Go play in traffic," said Maria. "You two are nothing but a couple of jerks." The boys laughed again and kept nudging her.

Two blocks away, Ben Secani was washing a car parked at the curb. He looked up when he heard the fuss and saw what was happening. He dropped the cigarette he was smoking, wiped his hands on his pants and then walked into the alley.

"Hey, let me help you carry your bag," said the boy on her left.

He slid his hand between Maria's stomach and the bag and pushed it upward, brushing his forearm fully against her breasts as his hand grabbed the bag.

"Stop that, you asshole."

She tried to hold onto the bag and spin away from the boy, only to bump into the other one, who repeated the other boy's tactic. He was too busy fondling Maria to notice Ben, who intercepted them, placed an arm around the boy's neck and applied pressure.

"Having a good time, fellas?" Ben said to them.

The other boy turned and ran full speed across the street and out of sight.

"Look, Mister, we were just having some fun," said the boy in Ben's grasp. "We don't want any trouble."

"What do you mean, *we?* Your partner hit the road."

Maria smiled at Ben.

Ben decided to teach this boy a lesson in economics. He spun the boy around and slammed him against the building. "There's nothing wrong with fun," said Ben. "I like to have fun, too. I go to the track lot, but it's not free. I have to pay to get my fun. It's time you learned that it costs."

"What do you mean?" The boy's voice cracked.

"This fun is going to cost you. Give me your money!"

"I don't have any money."

Ben slapped him hard across the face.

"Okay, okay," said the boy, trembling. He reached into his pants pocket and took out eighteen dollars. Ben grabbed the money and handed it over to Maria, who took it with an even bigger smile on her face.

"Hey, that's all I got," pleaded the boy.

Ben smacked him again. "Well, I don't think it's enough, but I'll let you off easy this time."

"That's not fair. What about Billy?" His voice cracked, realizing he shouldn't have mentioned the kid's name.

"I suggest that you see him about making him pay his share. Remember, if you or Billy ever want to touch this young lady again, it's going to cost you and next time eighteen bucks won't cover it. Now get lost."

The frightened boy turned away and ran in the same direction as the other one as Maria put the money in her pants pocket. "Thanks, Ben. I'm sure glad you came along. I wasn't in the mood for those two."

"You know them?"

"Yeah, Ronnie Canto and Billy Vittagliano, a couple of high school jerks. I know their younger brothers."

The names didn't mean anything to Ben. "I don't think they'll bother you again."

Maria's tone changed. "Please don't tell my folks about this, okay, Ben? Mom will just get pissed off at me like it was my fault for having boobs. Dad's got enough on his mind, trying to make ends meet. I don't want him worrying about me."

"I'll have to tell your dad, Maria. It's better that he hears it straight from me than from somebody else. He's a cool guy. I can smooth it with him. Besides, he's your dad. He should know what's going on around here."

"It's not like I was getting raped, for chrissakes. They were just feeling me up. They wouldn't have the balls to try anything else."

"Nice mouth. Where'd you pick that up?"

"Oh, please, Ben! You know my mom. Gee, you'd think I was a ten-year-old or something! You know, that wasn't such a hard way to make eighteen bucks!"

Ben laughed at Maria's remark. *She's some cool kid. She learns quickly, too,* he thought. "Get your little tail home, kid."

Maria giggled, clutching her bag, and headed quickly down the street to her house. Entering her house and dropping her stuff on a chair in the living room which faced the street, Maria stood still and listened carefully as she thought she heard the back door close.

"Mom, is that you?"

"I'm in the bathroom," called Anna Falcone from the downstairs half bathroom, located off the main hall.

Maria turned her head toward the direction of the sound. She heard the toilet flushing and then water running and finally the bathroom door opening. Her mom's footsteps led to the kitchen.

"Was there somebody here?" asked Maria, entering the kitchen. "I thought I heard the back door close."

"You're just hearing things, Maria. Go do your homework."

"I just got home, Mom. I need a snack."

Maria walked past her mother to get at a cookie jar on the counter and smelled the strong odor of whiskey. Two small glasses with ice melting in them sat in the kitchen sink. Maria grabbed a cookie and walked quickly back into the living room. She picked up her bag and headed for the front door.

"I'm going over to Gina's house. We're going to work on a project together. See ya."

Maria hoped her mother bought the story and also hoped that Gina, who lived close by, was home.

"Ah, go ahead," said her mother as she pulled one of the glasses out of the sink and refreshed her drink. "Don't be late for dinner."

Maria scooted down the street a half block and ran up the stoop to Gina's front door. She sighed with relief when her friend answered the doorbell.

"Hi," said Maria quickly. "I gotta come in, okay?"

"Yeah. Are you in trouble?"

"Nah. Can we go to your room?"

"Sure."

Gina called to her mom in the kitchen to let her know Maria was with her.

The girls settled into Gina's room and sat on the bed.

"You sure you're okay?" asked Gina.

"I'm okay. My mom's been drinking again. I just had to get out of there before she gets nasty with me."

"Boy, that's lousy, ya know, that she gets like that. You can always come over here."

"Thanks. I think she had a visitor, too. I heard someone go out the back door when I came in and I saw two booze glasses in the sink."

Gina's eyes opened wide.

"My dad doesn't buy a lot of booze but she always seems to have plenty. I bet her visitor gets it for her and I think I know how she pays for it," said Maria, her head turning to the side, as if she couldn't face her friend when admitting her suspicions about her mother.

Her friend quickly changed the subject. "Hey, wanna see something?"

Without waiting for an answer, Gina hopped off the bed and reached under the mattress. She pulled out a paperback novel that was worn and had wrinkled pages, a sign that it had gotten a lot of attention from young readers. The cover showed a couple in a tight embrace, the woman's dress ripped open across her back and the man nuzzling her neck.

Maria quickly flipped to a dog-eared page and read quickly to herself. "Oh, this is hot stuff," said Maria, as she flipped ahead to the next marked page. "If your mom ever finds this, she'll drag you down to confession before you can blink." Both girls laughed.

As Maria continued to flip the pages of the book, Gina spoke softly to her. "It must feel good to actually do it with a guy you like."

"There's one way to find out."

"Maria! I was just wondering. Hey, don't tell me you have . . ." her voice trailed off.

"Nah, not yet. As you said, with a guy you like. None of those creeps at school fill the bill."

"Then how are you gonna find a guy?"

"Maybe when we're sixteen we can get jobs after school. Then, with the money we get, we can hop on the *T* and scout out other places."

"That's a ways off. It'd be great if we could get some money sooner than sixteen."

"Yeah," said Maria looking up from the book. "It'd be great to be able to get some cash whenever we need something."

After two hours at Gina's house, and knowing that her father would be home soon, Maria reluctantly decided to leave. As she walked up the street to her house she saw her father's car pull up and park on the curb in front. Maria's spirits picked up quickly on seeing her dad. It would be better to enter the house with him.

"Maria," said Alberto, excitedly, as he got out of his car. "I've got something for you."

When Maria reached his side, he took a small book out of a bag in his hand and gave it to his daughter. "I know how much you like to read about Italy and ancient Rome, so I got you this. I'll probably read it, too, when you're done. But it's for you." Maria took the copy of *The Twelve Caesars* by Suetonius.

"Thanks, Daddy, I like paperbacks." Maria held back a snicker while thinking about Gina's book.

ffff

They went inside and Maria ran upstairs to put her things away. The Falcone house took on a more family-type atmosphere now that Alberto was home. He went into the kitchen and found his wife pouring water into a large pot. He wrapped his arms around her and kissed her on the cheek. "Hi, Baby."

"Hi," she answered without emotion.

Alberto smelled the odor of mouth wash on his wife's breath and his smile turned to a frown, knowing that she was trying to cover up the smell of whiskey again. "I'll go upstairs and wash up for dinner."

"Dinner will be ready in fifteen minutes. Tell Maria to come down here and set the table."

When he got upstairs, Alberto called to Maria. "Go help your mother, Maria." Maria sprang out of her room just in time to see her father's face before he turned toward the bathroom. His joy about the book was now gone.

After dinner, Maria helped her mother wash the dishes and Alberto settled into a recliner in the living room and lit up his pipe, anticipating a relaxing evening. A moment later the kitchen phone rang and Alberto heard his wife's voice greet the caller. "Oh, hello, Ben. Yeah, he's here. I'll call him. Maria, get your father. It's for him."

Before Maria could appear in the living room, Alberto was on his feet to meet her halfway down the hall.

"It's Ben Secani for you, Dad," said Maria, turning to walk with him into the kitchen.

Alberto entered the kitchen and took the handset from his wife with one hand while cradling his pipe in the other. "Hello, young fella. How are you? Go to Suffolk tonight? Sure, why not. Haven't been there in a long time.

But I'll just watch. Things are a little tight right now." Alberto caught a disapproving glance from Anna. "I'll meet you in front of your house in a few minutes."

Alberto hung up the phone and looked at Anna. "Ben wants me to go along with him to the track. I won't stay long."

Both of the Falcone women looked annoyed, Anna because Alberto got to go out and have fun while she had to stay home with Maria; her daughter because her Mom often got verbally abusive when her father was out.

Alberto grabbed a jacket and his blue Red Sox hat with the red letter B in the center. The race track was just over a mile away, and Alberto liked to walk there, keeping his car securely parked in front of his house. As he reached Ben's, he never broke stride as Ben got up from his seat on the stoop and joined him.

"Don't worry about the betting, Alberto, I got it covered, just like you used to do for me."

Alberto smiled and puffed on his pipe. "Okay. That's fair enough."

As they walked, Ben brought up the subject of Maria's experience earlier in the day. "You know, Alberto, your daughter's getting some attention from the boys in the neighborhood."

"Yeah, I'm sure she is."

"Today a couple of older boys got a little out of line when she got off the school bus."

Alberto pulled the pipe out of his mouth and looked at Ben.

"I was washing my car and saw them. Maria was pretty cool. She handled the thing real well. But I had to give them some discipline. It's okay." Ben waved his palms in the air. "I persuaded them that Maria is not their type. They got the message."

Alberto puffed on his pipe and looked straight ahead as they walked. "Thanks, Ben. I'm glad you were there to help. Maria's going to be a beauty. That can be a blessing and a curse."

"She can take care of herself. She's a sharp cookie."

"Yes, she is. I wish I could take her out of East Boston, but, what can I do? I hope she can get a scholarship for college. I don't think I'll be able to help much." Alberto's tone changed. "You're like a big brother to her, Ben. It's good of you to keep an eye out for her." Ben smiled and nodded as the two men continued on.

r r r r

Two years passed and Alberto's prediction about Maria was right. By sixteen, she was a beautiful young woman. She let her dark hair grow long and straight, and her figure filled out in perfect proportion to her five-foot, four-inch height. Although the boys in school were very interested in her, she dated infrequently and avoided becoming attached to any one guy.

An excellent student, Maria thrived in classes and was elected to the Student Council. She also did well at soccer, basketball and softball. With school and sports, a good part of her day was spent away from home. That was fine by her. Her home life became less and less happy. Her mother drank more often and there were always signs of male visitors in the house, like cigarette butts in the trash. Her dad only smoked a pipe and her mother didn't smoke at all, so these butts had to come from Anna's friends and she didn't have any female ones. The house often smelled of room refresher. When she got home, Maria spent most of the time in her room.

One fall night, even her room was not enough of an escape. Alberto was working late and Maria tried to do her homework while Anna shouted obscenities at her. Maria decided to go out to clear her head. She couldn't concentrate.

Still wearing the pleated green skirt and yellow blouse she had worn to school, she grabbed a sweater, moved quietly down the stairs and, when she got to the front door, she called out. "I'm going over to Gina's."

"Wha . . . what did you say? Get back here." But Maria was already out the door.

Anna just fell back into her chair in front of the television and mumbled to herself, "That little slut. The hell with her."

Maria stepped off her front steps, turning toward Gina's house. She walked quickly at first, then slowed down. She looked up at Gina's house and stopped. After a moment, she started walking again, slowly. Needing to be alone for a while, she just kept going along the sidewalk, past the row houses. In the fall darkness, she didn't notice the three young toughs in a four-door sedan parked on the opposite curb. The one sitting in the front passenger seat pointed to Maria and whispered to his friends. They nodded in agreement.

The guy in the backseat got out and crossed the street quietly as the car pulled out slowly and drove up the street. Maria walked farther until she got past the houses and reached a vacant lot adjacent to a small park with bushes that needed trimming and tall grass. The young punk who'd left the car walked quickly, closing the distance to Maria. Suddenly the car returned. It pulled up to the curb in front of Maria and the two other young men got out quickly and stood together on the sidewalk facing her. She stopped walking. Recognizing one of the young men, she knew she needed to get away. She turned to run and bumped right into the man following her. He grabbed her with one arm while another threw a rag around her face, gagging her with it and then tying it tightly around her head. Two men grabbed her arms and the third man grabbed her legs as they lifted her and carried her behind the bushes and deeper into the park. Maria had escaped her mother only to fall into another hell.

The punks held Maria down on her knees, taking her from behind. One held her head down in the grass with one hand and clutched her arm with the other. She couldn't move as the three took turns.

"Oh, no need to cry," said the one she'd recognized, his voice giving him away even more so, as Maria whimpered through the gag. "This is a big night for you. Consider it an initiation. Welcome to the big girls club. Now, nobody's gonna hit you or cut you up. We don't want to spoil that pretty face. And we don't want to leave any marks that would show, 'cause you're not gonna tell nobody about this. Get it? 'Cause if you tell anybody, we'll be back. And maybe we'll pay your family a visit, too. Just remember that."

Maria understood him plainly, and it made her feel helpless.

The three men finished with Maria and let go of her, reminding her to keep quiet. They adjusted their clothing and ran back to the sidewalk, then looked around as they walked to their car, got in and drove away. Maria fell onto her side and pulled the gag from her head, then slowly pushed it up her skirt; pressing it against her groin, weeping quietly.

Eventually Maria stopped crying and got to her feet. Dropping the rag, she pulled her panties back up, brushed off her skirt and walked back to the sidewalk. The air felt suddenly cold against her and she shivered slightly as she walked back home in the dark, gritting her teeth against the pain. She dreaded confronting her mother, but Anna, still in her chair in front of the TV, was asleep. Relieved, Maria slipped up the stairs and went into the bathroom where she tried to clean the night's filth from her body.

Chapter Eleven
1968

In the two years that followed Maria's horrible night, the lives of Ben Secani and Maria Falcone had changed considerably. Ben learned a great deal from his boss about how to make an illegal buck. His reputation as an effective executioner had grown throughout New England among the Mob leaders. He took on any job that was assigned to him and he managed to cleverly cover his tracks every time. He learned how to build layers of insulation between him and his targets and to use people to his advantage. His reputation also gave him greater access to women. He was a tall, handsome and tough young man who appealed to the dancers in Joe's club, and Joe let Ben have his pick of them whenever he wanted.

Things were very different in the Falcone home, too. Over a year had passed since the day Maria came home from school and found nobody home. Her mother had cleaned out her closet and dresser drawers and placed a note on her bed pillow. She didn't say who she was going with or where she was headed. She said she was sorry to do it this way, but she just couldn't take her dull life in the dreary old row house and the East Boston neighborhood anymore. She said that she was never cut out for motherhood and that Maria would be better off with just her father.

At first, Maria was stunned by the revelation that her mother had run out, but she was more confused than hurt. How could a woman be married for so long and then turn her back on her husband and daughter? What coldness can exist in a woman that would cause her to do it? What was so important about marriage if a couple can become so unhappy? On the other hand, her mother's abusive behavior would no longer taint this house.

Alberto Falcone's reaction was, on the surface, predictable. He knew that his wife was a failure as a wife and mother and had become a drunken adulteress. He knew that her departure was inevitable. He just didn't know when or how it would happen.

One evening after dinner, Alberto sat in the living room staring at nothing in particular. Maria entered the room and looked at him. Her eyes began to glaze over.

"Daddy, I miss your beautiful smile. I want to see you looking happy. You never seem to go out. Why don't you call Ben and go to the race track like you used to?"

"I really don't feel like doing that right now, sweetie, but thanks for thinking about me."

"You work late a lot more than you used to. I wish you came home earlier. And you're so quiet when you are home. You hardly ever talk to me anymore."

"I'm sorry, dear. I'm just tired when I come home."

One evening after dinner, Alberto told Maria that he was going to walk down to the corner market to get some pipe tobacco. It was raining lightly and fog was settling in off the ocean. Alberto put on an overcoat and hat and stepped out, closing the door quietly as if not wanting to add noise to an already very quiet house.

Maria was in her room deciding which of her homework assignments she'd work on first. She pulled the large literature book out of her bag and flipped to the section on the short story. Her assignment was to read a short story and write a brief analysis of it. She selected *Flight*, by John Steinbeck, which she had read before. Perhaps it should be titled *Escape*, thought Maria. Wasn't that what Pepe' was trying to do? Then she thought of her mother. There can be many reasons to try to escape.

The sound of a siren on the street annoyed Maria as it broke her concentration on the story. She shrugged it off and continued reading until she was interrupted again, this time by a loud knock on the door. She heard the knock again as she skipped down the stairs. A pulsating red light flashed through the front window of the living room as Maria peered through the peep hole of the front door. A police officer stood outside. "Is this the residence of Alberto Falcone?" asked the officer after Maria opened the door.

"Yes, is something wrong?" she asked.

"Are you a relative?" he asked.

"Yes, I'm his daughter. What's happened?" Maria's voice rose and her eyes opened widely, looking up the street at the ambulance.

"Miss, I'm afraid there's been an accident. Your father was struck by a car while trying to cross the street. The driver of the car said he stepped out of nowhere. I guess he wasn't paying attention to traffic."

Stunned, Maria collapsed in the officer's arms.

The funeral took place on a crisp October day with bright sunshine. When it was over, Maria received guests at her house. Betty Secani and some of the other neighborhood women helped prepare sandwiches and refreshments. Betty had made phone calls to notify Alberto's co-workers and the few friends he had, including her son, Ben.

Most of the guests paid their respects quickly and left after an acceptable period. Maria's friend, Gina, and her parents stayed a little longer. When they finally left, only Betty and Ben Secani remained. They sat in the living room, filled with the aroma of strong coffee from cups left on the coffee table.

"I want you to move in with me," said Betty. "You shouldn't be alone in this apartment. You're a senior in high school. You've got to be able to focus on your studies. Besides, my place has lots of room since Benny moved out. I'd love to have you. You can have his old room. You can even move in all your furniture, you know, your bed and desk. You can make it feel just like your own room."

"Yeah, no problem," said Ben. "I can get some help to move the furniture. Mom's right about this. It'll be best for you."

Ben hadn't seen much of Maria over the last year. He couldn't help notice how beautiful and shapely she had become. Maybe he'd have to stop by his Mom's place and visit more often.

"Thank you," said Maria. "You're very kind. Besides, I can't pay the rent."

"Don't worry about that. I'll talk to the landlord. We'll work something out," assured Ben.

Alberto carried a small life insurance policy with his employer, just enough to pay for his funeral expenses with only a few hundred dollars left for Maria. Moving in with Betty was the right course of action under the circumstances but Maria knew it had to be temporary. She would finish her senior year and graduate. It was time for Maria Falcone to become her own woman at a tender age.

Maria took a week off from school for the funeral and moved in with Betty as agreed. Ben showed up with a friend and they moved her bedroom furniture into Betty's house. Maria decorated the room much as it had been and felt comfortable in it. By week's end, Maria was ready to resume her schooling and move on with her life. The sadness remained at the loss of her father, but not the pain. She felt a strange sense of freedom that was new to her, but welcomed.

Betty helped Maria put an ad in the newspaper to sell off the remaining furniture in her father's row house. She also sold her father's old car. They brought in a small amount that gave Maria additional cash to go along with the remains of the insurance money. Money would become a problem eventually.

Betty did all she could to make Maria feel at home in her house and included her in the small Secani family's Thanksgiving and Christmas holiday observances. Maria, however, became withdrawn from adults and kept a respectful distance from Betty, despite her good intentions. She helped in preparing meals and cleaning the house, but never carried on a prolonged conversation with Betty. She did her schoolwork diligently and maintained her friendship with Gina. She was, in fact, a different person at school, being a good student and taking part in after school sports and activities, as though she was instinctively learning to lead two lives.

On a fairly mild winter night, Maria went over to Gina's house. It was more comfortable than being cooped up in her room and enabled her to avoid Betty Secani's annoying polite attempts at friendship. They sat on Gina's bed and worked on their Biology homework for a considerable time before Gina decided a break was needed.

"You want to see my other Biology book?" she asked Maria.

"Oh, oh!" exclaimed Maria. "What have you got now?"

Gina broke into an impish grin and slid off the bed. She went to her dresser and opened the bottom drawer, reached under the items of clothing and pulled out a paperback book. *The Hooker's Paradise* was a recent bestseller that detailed the experiences of a big city madam. "Oh, I don't believe it," said Maria. "Let me see! Let me see!"

"This is amazing," said Gina, lowering her voice. "I never imagined there were so many ways to, well, you know, to do it. And the money the guys paid for a night with some of these women! Some of their customers are famous people, at least that's the implication, although they don't name names. This is really cool!"

"Have you read the whole thing?" asked Maria.

"Yeah," said Gina. "You want to borrow it? Go ahead. But I need to get it back when you're through. I like to read over some of the good passages." Maria skimmed through the pages and Gina continued talking. "Some of the women entertain guys who set up dates, that's what they call them, in advance and the date takes them out on the town. Then they go back to a fancy hotel and they do it. The guy puts out some big money and the woman, well, she just puts out." Gina giggled and Maria smiled, shaking her head. For two teenage girls, this book was a real eye opener.

"Nothing quite like a little book learning," said Maria.

Gina looked down for a moment and then spoke in a serious tone. "Maria, I know it's really personal, but, well, have you done it yet? Are you a virgin?"

Maria looked up from the book, stared at Gina blankly and then looked back at the book. "No, I'm not a virgin," she said without emotion. "But, like you said, it's personal. I don't want to talk about it."

"Okay, okay," said Gina excitedly. "I understand. Really!" Gina was thrilled that her friend had taken the big step. Of course, she had no idea that it was involuntary.

"Well," said Gina, "I think I'm ready. I mean, I can't go off to college a virgin. I just can't!" Gina got more excited as she talked. "Of course, the problem is finding the right guy for it, you know?"

Maria looked up at her, realizing how serious her friend was about losing her virginity. "Have you got any candidates?" asked Maria.

"No, not specifically," Gina answered.

"What about Tommy Hunter, on the basketball team? You went out with him, didn't you?" inquired Maria. "How did that go?"

"He was okay," said Gina. We went out twice. He tried to feel me up on the second date, so I let him. Everything went okay, but he hasn't asked me out since then. Maybe he's too timid about going past that. Do you have any recommendations?"

Maria just shook her head negatively, but a little grin appeared on her face and then went away as quickly as it had appeared. She looked at her watch and then got up off the bed, reaching for her coat. "I'd better get going. I've got more reading to do," she said smiling as she put the book Gina gave her into her bag with her school books. "I'll see you tomorrow."

"Okay," said Gina. Gina walked down the stairs with Maria and followed her to the door.

"See ya," said Maria, as she went out the door and hurried down the street to Betty Secani's house, keeping her eyes straight ahead as she passed her family's old house. *Where could she find a candidate to deflower Gina?* she thought.

A few days later, Ben came over to his mom's house for dinner, something he tried to do once or twice a month to keep his mom happy and to look out for her. He was glad Maria was now a part of that equation, as he no longer saw her as Alberto's little girl. In the right hands, so to speak, she could be quite an asset to a guy.

Ben sat at the dinner table across from Maria as Betty brought in a large salad to go with the pasta already on the table. "Maria, give me your plate," said Betty. She took the plate and put a medium portion of pasta and two meatballs on it and then covered the meal with a ladle of sauce. Maria helped herself to the salad as Betty repeated the serving for Ben, only giving him a larger portion.

Ben opened a bottle of Chianti and poured a small amount for Betty and then a glass for himself. He stared at Maria and said, "What the heck. No reason why you can't have some here at home. What do you think, Ma?" Betty nodded. "Besides," said Ben, "You're eighteen now, so you're old enough, right?"

Betty reacted with surprise. "Oh, Maria, I'm so sorry. I didn't even think about your birthday. When was it?"

"It was three weeks ago," said Maria. "But don't worry about it. It's no big deal. Really! I don't want to make a thing about it."

"Okay," said Betty. "But I feel just awful about it."

"Please don't," urged Maria. "It's just a birthday."

Ben raised his glass and held it toward Maria. "Well, here's a belated happy birthday to Maria," he said, offering a toast. The three clinked their glasses and sipped the wine and then proceeded to enjoy their dinner.

"I can't remember feeling so good about anything as simple as having a family style meal in a loving home. Thanks to both of you."

After dinner Betty started to clear the table with Maria helping, but Ben intervened. "Ma, go sit down. We'll take care of this," said Ben, looking at Maria. Maria nodded with a smile.

"Okay, Benny, if you say so," answered Betty. In short order, the table was clear, the food put away and the dishes cleaned.

"How's that cute little car of yours?" asked Maria, opening up a conversation with Ben. "What kind is it?"

"That's an Austin-Healy. I got a good deal on it used over at Donati's garage. It needs some work, but it'll do for now. Someday I'm going to get my hands on a '56 T-Bird and get it fixed up. I'll have to save my pennies for that." Ben clearly liked his new toy.

"So, when are you going to give me a ride?" asked Maria.

Ben didn't answer immediately. He couldn't help but hear the possible suggestion in her words. "Eighteen, huh?" was his response.

"Yeah," she smiled back at him. Her look became more serious as she asked, "Am I old enough . . . for a ride?"

Ben didn't answer. He put his dish towel down and went into the living room where Betty was watching the television. "Thanks for the dinner, Ma," he said to her.

"Leaving already?" asked Betty.

"I'm going to take Maria out for a spin in my new car," he said.

"Don't keep her out long. It's a school night for her," instructed Betty.

"No problem," said Ben.

Ben went to the hall closet and got his coat. He motioned to Maria and she came over and got hers. They didn't speak as they went out the front door and got into Ben's car.

"This is nice," said Maria as she slid into the passenger seat and Ben closed the door for her.

"I think you're going to enjoy the ride," he said, and then walked around to the driver's side and climbed in.

Ben started the car as Maria watched and he drove out of the neighborhood. The mild winter had left the roads clear, but Ben left the top up, since it still was not convertible weather. He quickly made his way up Bennington Street and headed toward Eliot Circle.

"I like it," she said, smiling at Ben. "I'm going to need a car pretty soon myself."

"Why?" asked Ben. "You take the bus to school and can get around on the T, so what do you need a car for?"

"I'll be out of school pretty soon. I'll need my freedom."

"What about college?"

"I'm not going to college. I didn't apply anywhere. After Daddy died, I just didn't care much about it. Besides, I need to work for a while to put some money together. I might go to college in a couple of years. What's the rush? Maybe you can help me think of a good way to make some money."

Ben glanced quickly at Maria and then turned back to the road. Her skirt was short enough to reveal her shapely legs. He certainly knew some ways Maria could make money. Ben turned around at Eliot Circle and headed back south. Maria noticed that they didn't take the road back to Betty's house. She said nothing. He pulled into a neighborhood not far from his mother's house, but one that Maria never had been to before. Pulling up to the curb, Ben parked in front of a white clapboard house. "I thought you might want to see my place," said Ben. He stared at Maria and waited for her response. She waited momentarily before speaking, as if making an important decision, which she was.

"Yeah, I'd like that," she answered assuredly.

Ben climbed out of the Healey and walked around to Maria's side, opened the door for her and helped her out. He led her to a stairway on the side of the house that took them up to the main entry. They entered through a hallway and emerged in his clean, but unadorned living room. There was a comfortable-looking red sofa, an easy chair, two end tables with lamps and a television on a stand across the room. A coffee-colored carpet covered the floor wall-to-wall. "It's nice," said Maria. "But you could use some pictures on the walls."

"Yeah, well I haven't gotten around to that just yet," he replied. For the first time, Ben thought about the décor of his apartment.

He took Maria's coat and carried it with him as he walked into his kitchen. There he put both coats over a kitchen chair. "Care for a glass of wine?" he called to Maria.

"Sure, why not," she answered. Ben poured two small glasses of Chianti and carried them out to the living room. He handed one to Maria and held his out toward her. "Welcome to my pad," he said. She clinked his glass with hers and they each sipped their wine. Ben sat down at the end of the sofa and put his glass on the end table. When he turned back toward Maria, she had already taken a seat right beside him. Slightly startled by her closeness, but definitely pleased, Ben looked her over, sizing her body up from head to foot. He liked what he saw.

Maria smiled and looked at Ben, imitating the way he looked her up and down. She wanted to kiss him, but she waited. She sat still, looking up at him with her mouth slightly opened. Ben saw a woman, not a young girl, a woman who seemed to know how to conduct herself when alone with a man. He took her wine glass from her hand

and put it next to his own and then turned back to her. He placed his hand on the side of her face and pressed his lips slowly onto hers. She responded with a moist, soft kiss that begged for more. Ben's hand slid down from her face, caressing it slowly, and soon found her sweater. Maria sighed as Ben's hand cupped her youthful breast. She turned toward him in response, rubbing her knee against his leg. After another passionate kiss, Ben pulled his head back, breaking the kiss and looking straight into her eyes. He stood up and, taking both of her hands, he helped her up from the sofa. He held one hand as he turned and led her toward the bedroom door. She followed and watched as Ben opened the door. She ran her hand across his chest as she entered the room. Ben entered the room without turning on the light. This was a night he had known would eventually take place.

Later that night after Ben had taken her home, Maria said goodnight to Betty and went to her room. What a night it had been! Should she tell Gina about it? No. It was too personal.

Maria had mixed feelings about having sex with Ben. On the one hand, it was good to have had a positive sexual experience, which she hadn't been sure could ever happen to her. On the other hand, there were no violins playing in her head. It was with Ben Secani, a great guy to her, but one with a reputation that concerned her. The kids at school said he was in the Mob, that he could be involved in some real serious stuff. What kind of future could a girl have with him? He'd probably had sex with dozens of girls. She was probably just another notch in his belt.

Keep a cool perspective about this, she thought. *He's probably had many girls in his business. Maybe some girls are his business. Where do I fit in?*

Chapter Twelve
1966

Ben Secani's connection to the Boston Mob started after his Vietnam tour. He saw a fair amount of black market trading and had come to believe one didn't have to be in the military to engage in such lucrative pursuits.

He began to spend time in the Combat Zone, Boston's area for sleazy bars, prostitution and crime figures. Many of the bars were, in fact, owned by the Boston underworld.

One night, in such an establishment, a rugged-looking guy took offense at the amount of attention Ben was giving to a club dancer. The result was a fight that ended so fast it barely disturbed the customers around them. A blow from Ben to the man's Adam's Apple was all it took. The bar manager sat silently across the room.

Nothing else happened to Ben that night, but when he returned a few nights later and ordered a beer, the bartender delivered it and told him it was on the house. The man seated next to Ben swiveled his bar stool toward him. "I like the way you handled yourself the other night, quick and clean with minimal disturbance to my patrons. I'm Gus Botecelli. I run this club, among other things."

Ben expected the opposite treatment from the manager, so he felt relief at Gus' compliment. "I'm Ben Secani. My pleasure. Hey, I didn't mean any trouble, but that jerk was way out of line."

"I agree, Ben. That was nice work. Where'd you learn to handle yourself?"

"Well, I grew up in East Boston and picked up a few tricks compliments of Uncle Sam."

"Are you working?"

"I take some classes at the community college through the GI Bill. I do some odd jobs here and there to make some cash."

"Tell you what: I can set you up with a night job at the Dedham Envelope and Stationery plant. I have an interest there. It will be steady. I also hire guys from the plant for, as you call it, *odd jobs*. They're not the kind that appear in the classifieds, if you get my drift."

"That sounds okay to me. When do I start?"

"How about tomorrow night?"

"That's fine with me."

"Great. Come into my office. I'll give you the details."

Ben had great success with his new job and the money was very good. Some of the odd jobs gave Ben greater responsibility and soon he became so well-established that he was even hiring his own help from time to time.

One evening while Ben was buying coffee from a vending machine at the plant, a co-worker walked by and handed him a slip of paper. Ben didn't greet the man, but simply took the paper from him.

"That's a horse you oughta play," said the man, who smiled and kept walking.

Ben walked off to an empty corner and took the slip of paper out of his pocket. Instead of seeing a racehorse's name, Ben saw instructions to go out to the last bay at the loading dock. The bay door was closed, so Ben stepped out through the pedestrian door onto the paved area outside. There, he was greeted by Gus, the man who owned the bar in Boston. He had many types of businesses.

"Call in sick tomorrow night. It'll be good for you," said the man.

Ben smiled and looked at him.

"Get a guy who can drive a big rig," said the business owner.

"I can drive a rig."

"No. You'll have other duties, like persuadin' the driver to give up his rig. Be at this warehouse no later than ten o'clock. Park your car out of sight."

Gus handed Ben a paper with the address on it. "There'll be a truck carrying two-hundred televisions. Once you've persuaded the driver to take a hike, you and your partner drive the rig to Springfield to this address."

He handed Ben another slip of paper. "There'll be a man there named Gino. He'll unload it and give you an envelope. Take out your share, which is three grand. Pay off your driver whatever you want out of that. Bring the rig back. Ditch it close enough to your car so you can walk back without being noticed. Get rid of your help and take the envelope home with you and wait for a phone call the next day. By the way, there's a persuasion tool in your car's glove compartment."

Ben looked startled that someone had gotten into his car.

"Don't worry. I didn't have to smash anythin' to get in. I'm a little better than that. When you're all done, toss it in the Charles."

"Got it."

Gus walked away into the darkness, and Ben returned to his station in the factory, pleased he would be sick tomorrow night.

Ben had a couple of guys in mind for the job, and settled on a guy called Phil, who worked with him sometimes and was a little older than Ben, but not as bright. Ben always gave him good jobs with enough money to make it worthwhile.

On the designated night, Ben called in sick, picked up Phil and drove to the warehouse. They parked in a lot across the street a half mile away and walked to the warehouse loading dock, approaching from the perimeter of the lot and staying behind some trees. They climbed over a tall chain link fence, dropped to the ground and hid around a corner of the building. The truck's engine was running as the workers finished loading large cardboard crates marked Zenith onto the truck. The driver appeared from inside the warehouse, waved to the last man to empty his hand truck and walk back into the warehouse. As the bay door closed, Ben and Phil ran up to the truck. Ben poked a gun into the ribs of the driver and spoke softly.

"You've got company, pal. Be smart and keep quiet. Get in the back."

The startled driver did as he was told and Ben joined him as Phil climbed up into the driver's seat, put the rig into gear and eased it out of the warehouse lot.

"Let me have your driver's license," commanded Ben.

The driver complied, and Ben read the man's name and address out loud.

"James Caldwell, 125 Harris Avenue, Milton, Mass," said Ben. "I'll just keep this. You can tell the Registry that you lost it. Now, here's the deal. As long as you're smart, you won't get hurt, nor will anybody at 125 Harris Avenue, Milton, Mass. Understand?"

James nodded.

"Make yourself scarce for a while, be a good boy and you'll get your rig back in about three hours."

Phil pulled off to the side of the access road that led from the highway to the warehouse. They let James Caldwell out of the truck.

"Remember, Jimmy boy," said Ben. "Stay away from anybody who knows you and keep quiet. Your truck will be back in the general area later on. Stay quiet and stay healthy." With control of a rig carrying about forty thousands of dollars worth of televisions, Ben and Phil drove away and pulled off their assignment without a hitch.

Ben slept until after eleven the next day. He was just rolling out of bed when the phone rang. "How'd it go?" asked the voice. It was Ben's boss, Gus *The Boat* Botecelli, who'd given him the assignment two nights earlier.

"It went great. I've got your package. Just tell me how to get it to you."

"Meet me in the parking lot at Kelly Field in Hyde Park in an hour."

A few minutes after Ben pulled into the empty parking lot, a black sedan drove up beside him. Ben grabbed the big yellow payoff envelope and got into the black sedan beside Gus. Gus counted the money as usual.

"Nothing personal, Ben, but it's good business always to do an accounting."

"No problem. I understand."

Gus nodded in approval and looked straight at Ben, whose expression changed from a satisfied smile to serious. Gus had something important on his mind.

"I'm glad you didn't have to use that piece I gave you, but if something goes wrong I want to know I can count on you to eliminate the problem. You've been doing good work, running important errands and such and jobs like last night. I need someone who can help me with some other duties . . . let's call it enforcing my business policies. It can get rough. I'm hoping you're up to it."

Ben lifted his chin slightly, but avoided the temptation to smile. He knew this was a promotion, of sorts, and that it meant he had earned a higher level of trust from Gus and his boss. "I was in some pretty messy stuff in 'Nam. Yeah, I'm up to it."

"Yeah, but over there you were supposed to kill people. Here, if you have to take somebody out, you're not supposed to get caught. That's bad for business. So, you gotta learn to do it cleanly. Of course, most of the time, you don't have to go that far, maybe just bust somebody up, but when the time comes, you gotta do the job."

"I understand, Mr. Botecelli. I can do whatever you've got."

"Good," said Gus. "You're not working at the stationery plant anymore. You'll find this job rewarding enough. And call me Gus."

Ben exited the car and Gus drove off.

He began working at new assignments for Gus *The Boat*. Among those assignments was collecting protection insurance payments from merchants in the Combat Zone and along the South Shore. Gus was a good boss and he allowed Ben some freedom in expanding the business. That pleased Ben.

The money was good, and Ben liked the feeling of power that rushed through him when he collected for Gus. It reminded him of the day he took eighteen bucks off the young punk who got fresh with Maria Falcone a couple of years ago. Only this was even better.

A few miles north of Suffolk Downs, the boulevard near Revere Beach, a Texaco gas station did a brisk business. Of particular note among the clientele were a number of trucks from a local yogurt distributor. The drivers used the Texaco station as their filling-up place and they seemed to be very familiar with the station owner, they just called Burt, popular because he offered the drivers and many other locals a chance to make a few dollars on the side. Burt made book out of his gas station and took bets on the horses, performing this community service without interference from the police, because many of them also filled their tanks with Texaco. It was profitable, and Gus *The Boat* had it in the grasp of his *insurance* business.

One afternoon, Burt was in the office eating his lunch and an assistant was pumping gas for the few customers coming by. It was normally slow that time of day, but it would pick up in the late afternoon when the yogurt trucks would pull in to fuel up for the next day. Two men walked into the shop while their car was being fueled and Burt looked up while finishing a bite, not recognizing them. Business was about to change for Burt, and for Ben Secani, too.

"Afternoon," said Burt. "Can I help you?" Something about these two told Burt trouble was in the air.

"The question is," said the taller of the two, "how we can help you?"

The man speaking wore a long black raincoat while the other had on a short warm up jacket.

"I don't follow," said Burt.

"Well, we know you have a very prosperous business here," said the raincoat. "But this is a very dangerous neighborhood. Heaven forbid that harm should come to such a business. So, our boss has authorized us . . . let's say you've been prequalified . . . for a very good insurance program."

Burt knew this game but couldn't believe that it was being played on him, again.

"Are you crazy or something? I don't think you know the score here."

The raincoat cast a quick glance at his partner. "I don't think you know the score, pal."

At that moment, the shorter guy in the Red Sox jacket produced a baseball from his pocket and fired it hard at Burt, hitting him in the stomach.

"Nice pitch!" exclaimed the tall man, who quickly retrieved the ball and flipped it back to his partner.

Burt doubled over in pain, grasping his midsection and looking back up at his assailants. The tall man spoke again.

"We'll be back tomorrow to pick up the first insurance premium, a mere two thousand dollars, cash. We know you can afford it. I'm sure your friends in the yogurt business would agree."

Burt rubbed the painful spot on his body and began to breathe better as the two men walked out of his station. This was going to get rough.

Later that day, Gus Botecelli sat in Joe Vito's office in the Club 77, relaying a call from Burt's Texaco to his boss.

"Check with your guys," said Joe. "Find out who these jerks are, trying to move in on my territory."

"I've already made some calls," said *The Boat*. "The descriptions don't fit anybody we know. They could be working for the Somerville guys or possibly some assholes trying to go independent."

"Who'd be that dumb, some unconnected punks stepping into something already taken? They don't know what they're doing. What did you tell the station owner?"

"I told him to make the payment tomorrow. We need some time to figure this out."

"Put somebody on this you can trust. I don't want you getting too close. There could be something funny going on."

"I got a good guy for this. He's young and tough. You wouldn't want to go one-on-one with him."

"Fine. I just hope he understands that nobody's bullet proof."

Ben hung up the phone after a conversation with Gus and headed for the address in the North End he'd been given. He parked in the back lot off the alley as instructed and slowly got out of his car. He put his hands in his coat pockets and leaned against the driver's side door.

"Over here," called Gus from a backdoor entrance.

Ben followed him through the door and up the stairs into an apartment. A man with thin, dark hair met them. He was wearing a shiny Celtics jacket.

"The place is yours, Gus," said the man.

Gus nodded and the man smiled at him and Ben, then left through the front. Seeing the quizzical look on Ben's face, Gus explained his business relationship with Charlie Senatori and why there were no introductions.

The two men moved into a large room with a round table and a bar in the corner. Gus poured two bourbons over ice and carried them over to the table. Following Gus's lead, Ben sat down and took a sip.

"I've got a special job for you, Ben."

Ben's eyes opened wide as he realized this must be the type of thing Gus had told him about that day at Kelly Field.

After filling Ben in, Gus said, "Once we know who these guys are, then we can act. I think it's Bellino's guys. He's in Somerville, Winter Hill." He took a drink, as if fortifying himself for the rest of the talk.

"They might be independents," he went on, "but I doubt anyone is that stupid. If it's Bellino, then one of two things is gonna happen. He's either gonna admit it or deny it. If he admits it, then we gotta be careful. That means he's makin' a bold territory move and will expect us to fight back. He's ready for that, I'm sure. We'd have to bump this up to the man in Providence. He wouldn't like to see an all-out war take place. If he denies it, then, whether he's lyin' or not, we take out the two jerks. It means either they are independents, or Bellino doesn't have the muscle for a war. We can put an end to it right there."

Ben swallowed a drink and sat back in his chair. He was feeling a rush like nothing he had felt since going out on patrol in Vietnam. Gus finished his instructions.

"Take this," he said as he took a handgun with a silencer attached to it from out of his coat pocket and slid it across the table to Ben. "Got a handkerchief?"

"Yeah."

"Wipe it down."

Ben took out a handkerchief.

"I want you to get in the habit of doing this. Always wipe down the piece after you get it and after you use it. Then find a body of water, somethin' deep, and toss it in. Don't always use the Charles River. It's getting polluted." They both laughed.

"Stay home tomorrow. It's sometimes just as important to lay low before a job as well as after. At four o'clock, call this number. When the time is right, you'll get more instructions. If you bring in some help, you pay out of your money. Remember what I told you, the idea is not to get caught."

Ben nodded and gulped down the rest of his bourbon. He left his meeting with Gus and drove home quickly. He felt like electricity was flowing through his veins.

Ben needed an energy outlet when he got to his apartment. He quickly changed into exercise shorts and a cut off T-shirt and went into a bedroom that served as a catch-all room for him. Included in his collection of things was a set of dumbbells. Ben loosened up for a minute and then squatted down, being careful to bend at the knees, clutched the weights and stood up straight. He began doing biceps curls, alternating hands, left then right. He performed a series of biceps lifts and then switched to exercises that targeted other muscles. Ben's workout continued for over thirty minutes, without rests between exercises. He stopped when he had worked up a heavy sweat and was breathing hard. The workout served its purpose. Ben showered and dressed and finally relaxed while his mind focused on making a special phone call tomorrow at four o'clock.

The next day was damp with a light rain that let up in the afternoon. Gus Botecelli stood alone near a public phone in the empty parking lot at the base of the Blue Hill ski area in Canton. After glancing at his watch, he stepped inside the booth. In a minute the phone rang and Gus answered it.

"Is the party on?" asked Ben.

"I need to help you with the guest list. Meet me at 1200 Beacon Street in twenty minutes. We'll work it out."

Bellino had been approached through proper channels and denied having anything to do with the move on Burt's Texaco. It was a go for Ben. Over a week went by, as per *The Boat's* instructions. The plan was to let the two guys collect a payment from Burt, hoping it would give them a false sense of security. If Bellino was lying, then he knew his boys were in for a hit and he couldn't do anything about it. If they were really working independently, then they were about to learn a lesson; a very final one.

Burt went about his duties at the gas station while his employee pumped gas for customers on the day when the two collectors came back, wearing the same coats as before. They pulled up to the pump and asked for a fill-up, as before, and then both men went inside the station.

"Good afternoon," said the man in the raincoat.

Burt looked up, keeping a straight face. "I got your money."

"Good. Because if you didn't that would be stupid and you don't look like a stupid man to me."

"In there," said Burt, motioning to the mechanic's bay. "Go right in."

It was empty, but smelled of oil, grease and rubber. A few tires lay on the floor in the corner. Burt walked across the floor to a tool cabinet with a lock on the door. It hung on the wall above a work bench. The two collection men stopped at the entrance to the bay and looked it over before following Burt in. Some coveralls lay in a pile on the floor to the right of the entrance and a tarp was crumpled up on the floor beside them. The men walked past them, but stopped after just a few feet, keeping some distance between them and Burt. They focused on him as he unlocked the tool cabinet. Burt pulled a tool box off the shelf and put it down on the work bench. He opened it and took out a large yellow envelope that bulged with its contents. The man in the raincoat motioned to Burt to bring it to him.

Burt hesitated.

"Something wrong?" asked the tall man.

"No, no." He stepped up to the men and handed over the envelope. "That's all of it."

As if on cue, a swishing sound followed Burt's words and he dropped to the floor. The two men fumbled for their weapons, dropping the envelope. Ben Secani appeared from under the tarp that lay behind the men.

Pop. Pop. Pop. Pop.

Four crisp sounds and the two collectors went down before they could reach their guns. Ben quickly rifled through each man's pockets, taking some cash from each. He slid their guns back into their holsters after making sure each man was dead.

Burt got up to his hands and knees, breathing heavily, his eyes wide open. Being a bookie had its risks, but he had never been close to anything like this. It was his first execution, too. Ben took the tarp that had been his hiding place and spread it out on the floor beside the dead men. He piled them on to the tarp, one on top of the other, and folded it around them.

"You got some twine?" Ben asked the shaken Burt. He nodded and got a spool from a hook on the wall.

"Help me tie this off." The two men tied the tarp tightly around the corpses, closing it off at each end. "Go get the car. Back it in."

With the car in the garage bay, Ben opened the trunk and he and Burt placed the bound up bundle inside.

"Clean this up," Ben said, motioning toward the blood on the floor. "Then burn the rags."

Ben went into the station office and made a phone call. The gas station attendant came into the garage bay and stopped at the opened door, standing next to the front end of the car. Burt waved him off and the young man nodded, then went back to the gas pumps. He understood.

Without speaking any further, Ben got in the car, started the engine and drove away. His plan for disposing of the bodies was set and his contact knew where to meet him. Ben Secani had begun his career as a hit man in the Boston Mob.

Chapter Thirteen
1968

Maria started job hunting before her high school graduation day. She didn't want any of the usual summer jobs available to kids. She searched the want ads in the Tribune for something permanent, but didn't expect much. After a few days of reading the ads, she saw something that looked good. It said *office assistant,* which she knew was a euphemism for secretary, but that was all right. She was a good typist, and the job was located at the Prudential Center. That meant she could get out of East Boston for most of the day and be working in one of the most exciting places in the city of Boston. There were shops and restaurants and lots of business people, a higher class of individuals than those who hung around on the streets of East Boston. And it would be an easy commute on the T.

Maria got the job at Hatten Agency, located on the twenty-third floor of the Pru. By mid-June, she had settled in nicely on the job. She helped Peg Eaton, Mr. Hatten's secretary, with her clerical duties, freeing up Peg to work more closely with Mr. Hatten in running the agency. She also had to back up Joan Salisbury at the receptionist's desk for breaks and during Joan's vacation. Although neither of the two women made any attempt to become friends with Maria, Peg at least gave her an occasional pat on the back for good work, while Joan was always gruff and acted as though she didn't want Maria around at all. It reminded Maria of her mother. Perhaps her family life was an accurate sample of the larger adult world. Perhaps Joan had pain in her life she transferred to others.

When Maria started at Hatten, there were two women agents. By mid-summer, there was only one left. Her name was Gloria Swenson, twenty-three years old; she had been with Hatten for two years. She came to the agency right out of Babson College where she studied Marketing. She told Maria that the job required basic sales skills. Gloria was a natural at it.

The two young women became friends and often took lunch together. One afternoon they went to a popular Chinese restaurant on the ground floor of the Pru. They sat opposite each other in a booth not far from the main entrance where they could see patrons coming and going. Maria usually brought her lunch from home, so it was a treat to go out for lunch with a co-worker.

"I like getting away from the brown bag lunch now and then," said Maria. "But I couldn't do this every day. That can get expensive, especially on my salary, not to mention the extra calories. How do you manage?"

Gloria smiled and sipped her water. "I eat light. That keeps down the expense and the calories. I work out, too, just to keep my figure. After all, a girl's got to take care of her assets." Both women laughed.

"You don't look like you ever have to worry about that."

Gloria was a little taller than Maria and had a slim, attractive figure. "Well, I just want to make sure. I don't have to work too hard to keep trim, but I'd sure like to have a pair like yours."

Maria chuckled. "They can get you a lot of attention." Maria looked down at her breasts. "That's the good news. The bad news is that they can get you a lot of attention."

Gloria nodded in agreement and sipped her water again. The women ordered their lunches and continued talking.

"The first time I learned that lesson about guys being attracted to a girl's boobs was in junior high," said Maria.

"You had boobs in junior high? I didn't have that problem."

Maria went on to tell Gloria the tale of the time she was bothered by two schoolboys while on her way home one day. She told her how Ben Secani came to her rescue and made the creepy kid pay her eighteen dollars, all the money he had on him, for touching her breasts. Maria's look changed from amused to curious. A slight grin emerged on her face. She'd remembered something.

89

"I told Ben what had just happened wasn't the toughest way to earn eighteen bucks."

"You can't be making a lot in your current job, Maria. Why don't you try being an agent? You're smart and well spoken. And I could help you out. You ought to think about it."

"No, I don't think that would be right for me. The whole idea of having to ask someone to buy something leaves me cold."

"You'd be surprised. The idea is to have something they want. Find a need and fill it. In this business, we have guys who need jobs and we have employers who need workers. You just have to bring them together. I'll tell you, Maria, there isn't a walk of life that doesn't call for sales skills. You're either selling a product, a service or yourself." Gloria laughed. "I didn't mean it quite like that, not like the girls in the Combat Zone, that kind of selling yourself. But there are many ways to make good money. I like what you said to your friend, Ben, back then. It wasn't the toughest way to make eighteen bucks. That was cool!"

Maria smiled at Gloria and sat back as their food was delivered.

"So, all these years later, what became of your rescuer? Do you see him, go out with him?"

"Who, Ben? Now and then. Nothing steady. He's got other girls. I know that, so I'm not trying for anything steady. But a woman has her needs to address and I've always felt comfortable and safe with him. I have to be careful, though, since I live with his mother, Betty."

"No kidding! That sounds like a tricky situation."

"Yeah, it is. I usually meet him outside and then we go out to dinner or something and then we end up at his place. Then he takes me home. We keep it cool and nobody gets hurt. Neither one of us wants to get too close."

"I hear you."

Maria's tone changed and her eyes looked far away. "Some guys think they can take whatever they want from a girl, so they do and if she gets hurt, too bad. They want to show they've got control over you and the trouble is, sometimes they do. You can't always have a protector around." Maria looked back toward Gloria, regaining control. "I'm sorry. I guess I drifted off."

"Don't apologize. I understand. If you ever want to talk about it, I'm here."

There was a silent moment and each woman sipped some water, then Gloria put both of her hands on the table, palms down, as if she were getting ready to speak profoundly.

"A time comes for a girl when she realizes that she can't always be letting men take from her. She has to find a way for her to be the one who does the taking. Making it in a man's world is one way that works for me. I'm the only successful woman agent at Hatten. There have been other gals, but they come and go. Most of them have no idea what they're getting into. That's true of the guys, too. I'm more successful than most of the men up there and that sticks in their gut. And soon they're gone. There are only a handful of us who can do this well enough to make some dough. I intend to become the top earning agent at Hatten someday and then see what they offer me. If it's not as good as what they'd offer a man, then I'll move on, maybe start my own agency. I intend to call my own shots. And take from them. They're not going to take from me! They'll only get what I want to give them." Now it was Gloria with emotion in her voice. "Excuse me, Maria. I was getting a little carried away."

Maria sat back, lifting her head slightly, taking in all of what Gloria had to say. "No, not at all. You're right. You're absolutely right. I admire your strength. I can just see it, you owning your own agency, with a man servant, too!" They both laughed out loud.

"How about you?" asked Maria. "Do you have a steady guy?"

"No. I'm too busy. Let's just say my career comes first. Like you, I get my needs taken care of, but I don't have room for a romance."

Maria looked puzzled. "By career, you mean the Hatten Agency?"

"That's just a day job."

"Do you moonlight?"

"I have other interests. I'll tell you about it sometime. We need to get back."

The women finished their lunch and paid their checks. Maria noticed Gloria left a healthy tip.

"Really, Maria, you need to branch out if you want to make some decent money. Maybe I can help." The women marched toward the elevators.

Maria enjoyed being with Gloria. She was her first female friend who knew about the adult world and was close to her own age. Perhaps she could learn from her.

A week later, Maria did indeed get a lesson from her colleague and friend. Gloria stopped by Maria's desk and asked her to have dinner at her apartment. Maria agreed and the two left the building together. Maria was impressed that Gloria had her own car and parked it in the garage under The Pru. It was a dark blue Chrysler New Yorker four door sedan with leather interior.

They drove down Brookline Avenue to Boylston Street and turned in to The Village Square, a recent development in Boston that featured a high-rise apartment building, with restaurants and shops at the ground level. Gloria pulled into another below-ground garage with spaces for residents and some visitors. They took an elevator to the first floor of residences above the shops.

Gloria's apartment had two bedrooms, a kitchen and dining area separated by a counter and a large living room with wall-to-wall carpeting. It held a sofa, loveseat and a big swivel recliner, all upholstered in a matching green pattern. A glass top coffee table sat in front of the sofa. A twenty-five inch console television was in the far corner. Beside it were tall speakers attached to a Kenwood sound system, with a tuner, a turntable and a large reel-to-reel tape recorder.

Gloria slipped on an apron and gave Maria a glass of wine while she prepared the food. Maria offered to help and began preparing a salad. Soon they were dining on baked boneless chicken breasts and rice pilaf, along with the salad.

The women talked about the Hatten Agency to some extent, movies they had seen recently and their musical likes and dislikes. Eventually, Maria couldn't contain her curiosity any longer. "Gloria, this is such a beautiful apartment! And you have that nice, new car, wow! Maybe I should think about becoming an agent."

Gloria smiled. "The Hatten Agency allows me to earn a very good income, that's true. I almost make enough to be able to afford this place."

Maria looked puzzled. "Almost? I don't understand."

"Maria, remember our conversation at lunch last week? I told you that my position at Hatten is a day job. You asked me if I moonlight. Well, yes, I do."

Gloria took a sip of her wine, then looked at Maria. "I also said that a gal can't always be letting men take from her, that she has to find a way to do the taking."

Maria nodded.

"There are men in this town, very wealthy men, and they are used to taking things they want. So, I give them what they want, but they don't take it. They have to pay."

Maria sat silently.

"Are you shocked?"

"Yeah, sort of, but I'm also impressed. You're in such control of your life. How did you . . . get started?"

"I was in college and I got to be friendly with the Administrative Dean, a woman. I won't go into details. Let's just say she was my mentor. I needed money and not just enough for tuition. I wanted a lifestyle change. I'm not saying this is for any other girl. I'm just saying that I really meant what I told you at lunch. You have to be in control. You have to be able to take as well as a man. You may find some other way, something that is right for you. This is right for me. It's not legal, of course, so I don't intend to do it forever. I'm building up a nest egg that will make me financially independent. I'll always be able to call my own shots, perhaps as a VP at Hatten or as the president of my own business. Then I'll be living on the top floor, not just above the shops."

Maria sat back in her chair, holding her wine. "And you cook up a pretty good dinner."

The women finished the meal, talked and drank some more, and then Gloria called a cab for Maria and gave her more than enough cash to cover the fare. Maria thanked her and digested Gloria's words as well as her dinner the rest of the evening.

The weeks went by quickly and Maria realized the summer was racing past. But this year she didn't have a summer job. Her position at Hatten was permanent, so she had to think for the longer term.

One night at home in her room, she took out the copy of *The Hooker's Paradise* that she had borrowed from Gina. She read through several passages but with a different perspective this time. When she first got it from Gina, she saw the book as fun, something that would shock Betty Secani right out of her shoes. Now, after talking to Gloria, she consumed the text. The story of a woman who became a high priced call girl seemed to echo Gloria's words about calling your own shots and taking from men, rather than letting them take from you. The idea was to find something they want. Find a need and fill it. Maria thought she'd learned early on that she had what men wanted. They had the need and she could fill it. Close the sale. That's what Gloria had learned.

Living with Betty Secani was getting difficult for Maria. It wasn't that Betty was hard to live with, like her own mother had been. But Maria was starting to get anxious to get out on her own. Gina was going to leave for college in Maryland soon and couldn't contain her excitement. Maria was developing the urge to leave.

One evening after dinner with Ben and Betty, Maria suggested to Ben that they take a walk around the neighborhood.

"Ben, you know, living with your Mom has been great and I really appreciate what she's done for me."

Ben turned his head toward her while they walked.

"But I'm really getting anxious to get my own place. I'd love to get an apartment over in the Back Bay. I'd be close to work and it's a really great part of the city. But the rent is a bit steep for me. I don't know when I'll be able to afford it."

Ben knew a shakedown when he saw it. After all, that was his line of work. Now he knew he was about to be put on the receiving end, without the muscle. "Oh, I think I feel a hand in my pocket. Only this time it's reaching for my wallet!" Ben broke out laughing and Maria slapped him playfully on the shoulder.

"You're awful sometimes. Really, maybe you could help me. I'm not looking for a handout. You must know of ways that I could make extra money."

"Easy kid, be careful where you're going."

Maria paused and thought for a moment before continuing. "Look Ben, I'm a big girl now. I don't need to be sheltered. I know you make your living in what you might call unconventional ways."

Ben stopped her there. "Don't be too sure about what you think you know about me. Go on with your pitch."

"I'm okay with whatever you do. I see it this way. My dad worked hard all his life and where did it get him? A drunken wife who played around and an early grave, that's what he got. There's nothing wrong with taking care of yourself and if you have to find—let's call it a socially unacceptable way of doing it—then so be it."

Ben looked at her, but kept quiet. Maria knew she had gotten deeper into his life than she ever had before. They were connecting.

"So you think you're ready for some . . . unconventional business? What did you have in mind?"

Maria waited before speaking. She wanted to be sure she expressed herself in the clearest way without getting on Ben's wrong side.

"I know there are men in any city who like to have the pleasure of a young woman's company without their wives knowing about it. Not a mistress. Nothing complicated. They call and set up a time. They go out. She gives him a good time and he pays and pays well. I'm betting you know about that kind of man in this city. If I had my own place, I could occasionally entertain them and we could split the money, since you'd be paying for the apartment and connecting me to them."

Ben was absolutely astounded, but he didn't want to show it. Little Maria Falcone had grown up and she wanted to become a call girl. *Holy shit!*

"Are you sure you know what you're talking about?"

"Yes, I am. Let's be straight with each other. We have fun together, but we're not ever going to be talking marriage or a house in the suburbs with a white picket fence and a puppy. I'm making you a business proposition, one that would benefit both of us very well.

Now, if I'm wrong about your connections to important men in this city, then forget everything and I'll never suggest it again. But if I'm right, then there's money to be made for both of us. What do you think?"

Ben shook his head in disbelief. He would never have dreamed such an opportunity would fall right in his lap, certainly not from Maria. He knew from experience that she didn't look like an eighteen-year-old when she was dressed up to go out. She was a great looking girl with all the right equipment. She could command a healthy fee for services rendered. Of course he'd have to give a share to his boss, Gus *The Boat*. Money made is money shared, or you might come up short a couple of fingers.

Maria sensed a closed deal. "You can make the ground rules, Ben."

Maria felt strange after saying that. Of course Ben would make the rules. This was a man's world, Ben's world. She thought of Gloria's words. She was going to make it big in a man's world. That was bound to upset some people along the way, but as long as she didn't upset Ben, she would be safe. He looked at her.

"You're right. I don't like puppies."

Chapter Fourteen
1974

Frank Damone drove into the parking garage near the Sears store at the South Shore Plaza, parking on the first level. It was a sunny day, but Frank wanted the shade of the garage to keep his car cool. He'd separated a lot of cash from the beverage company and wanted to spend some of it on his wife and kids. The garage was about half full.

He pulled into a space nose-first against an inside wall and shut the engine down, took some cash out of the briefcase on the passenger seat and eased out of the dark blue BMW. Frank never noticed the three young men sitting in a beat up Dodge Dart several spaces away.

He'd no sooner locked the car door when he heard a voice say, "Gimme da keys." Frank turned around and saw three teenagers surrounding him. The one who'd spoken looked at Frank. Another eyed the BMW while the third scanned the garage.

"Hey, I don't want any trouble, so sure, you can have the keys." Frank tossed them hard at the kid's face, who tried to guard himself with his hands. Frank saw his chance and kicked the kid in the groin. He turned to the second assailant and threw a punch that glanced off the guy's chin. They were suddenly in a clinch and both fell to the ground. Frank landed on top, grabbed his opponent by the throat and slammed his head against the garage floor. He was about to do it a second time when he felt a sharp pain in his back, then another. Frank couldn't move. A third blow from the punk with the knife ended Frank's fight.

"Whatta we gonna do now?" cried the kid who had stayed back from the fight.

The leader grabbed the keys off the floor and got into the BMW. "We get outta here now."

"What about Jamie?"

"I think he's dead. Let's go."

The two sped away in the BMW, leaving their friend, Frank and a jackknife behind. It wasn't long before a shopper came on the scene and alerted Security. The Braintree Police showed up shortly after that and closed off the crime area. Frank was dead, but Jamie was still breathing.

The MET Police Dispatch heard the call about the incident and sent the word to the homicide department.

"Hey, Jack," said Leo. "That's the guy I talked to at South Shore Beverage, Frank Damone. He took over the business after Bertoli got killed."

"Coincidence?"

"Possible. But this sounds like a car theft gone bad."

"Or maybe that's what somebody wants it to look like. We'd better check it out."

Jack and Leo arrived at the Braintree incident and surveyed the site after identifying themselves to the on-scene commander. Frank's body was being taken by the coroner and Jamie was lying on a gurney, about to be sent to the nearest hospital.

"We tried to talk to the kid, Detective, but he's pretty groggy. He has a bad head wound, like he was getting it smashed against the garage floor by the victim," said the commander to Jack. "There's a small blood spot where he was lying out cold. There's a separate pool of blood around the guy who got stabbed, three times in the back. We have a couple of witnesses who saw a dark BMW with two young guys speeding out of the garage around the time Security got the call. I guess they weren't too concerned about their buddy, so they left him."

"Nothing like a robbery gone bad to help you find out who your friends are," said Leo.

"So you guys know the victim," said the commander. "Must be a Mob guy if you're interested."

"Where's the knife?" asked Jack.

"Our guys took it to the lab."

"We'll need your report when you have it."

"Done, Detective."

"Any ideas on these punks?"

"Well, there's that Dodge Dart over there. Seems to be abandoned. We'll check that for prints, too. It's possible they were staking the garage out, waiting for a good target, a car they wanted. A Beemer sounds like a good choice."

"I guess the auto theft ring is reaching out from the city," said Leo. "Makes sense. This mall has a huge parking area. These garages catch a lot of cars owned by upwardly mobile types, the kind of wheels that attract attention."

"You're right, Detective. We've had an increase in professional auto theft in the past year. The ringleaders recruit young punks to do the snatching, pay them well and there usually isn't any trouble. The victim is so scared he just gives up the car and runs off or stands there crappin' his pants while the thieves get away."

Jack walked over to the Dodge while the commander was talking. He looked inside and then went around it completely. The body had several dents in it with paint scratches that looked new. "If this was their car, it's probably stolen. Most Dart owners take good care of them. They last a long time if you don't go crashing them into things like somebody did with this. A shame."

Jack gave his card to the commander. "When you find out if the kid's prints or those on the knife match any in the Dart, let me know right away."

"You'll be hearing from me, Detective."

"Thanks."

The next morning, Jack got the call. The prints on the knife matched some found on the steering wheel and driver's door on the Dodge Dart, which was a stolen vehicle. Jamie's prints were found on the door handle in the back.

"I think the Damone murder is a dead end for us," Jack said, while Leo poured a cup of coffee. "Those kids definitely used the Dodge Dart to get to the garage, the prints confirm it."

Leo held a paper with more information and waved it at Jack. "And Jamie turns out to be James Leland Ford, eighteen years old, from Dorchester. Not much on him. He did a little time in Juvenile for petty theft. Guess he was tryin' to break into the big time. When do you want to pay him a visit?"

"Right now."

They drove to the hospital in South Weymouth where James Ford was recuperating from his injury, under police guard. The patient was awake in his bed. He turned away from his visitors when he saw Jack and Leo enter his room. They had cop written all over them.

Jack made the introductions and Leo walked around to the opposite side of the bed. "Don't be rude, Jamie. You're not in our jurisdiction."

"So why are you here?"

"We just need to clear something up. Why did you target Frank Damone yesterday?"

"I don't know any Frank Damone."

"Come on, Jamie. The guy you killed while trying to jack his Beemer, Frank Damone, why did you go after him?"

"Hey, I didn't kill nobody. That guy was trying to kill me. He jumped me and knocked me down in that garage. He started bangin' my head on the ground. That's all I remember. Next thing I know, I'm in here."

"Jamie, the Braintree Police have got you dead to rights on this one. You can play your game with them. We just want to know why this particular guy."

"I told you I don't know the guy. He had a nice car, that's all, a dark Beemer. I like those. I was just lookin' at it."

Leo leaned down toward Jamie. "Just lookin' at it, huh? Well, your friends liked it enough to steal it and leave you behind. How does that feel?"

"What friends? I was there alone, just lookin' at this car and the guy hits me."

"No, Jamie. Your fingerprints put you in the backseat of the Dodge. Kinda hard to drive from there. You were a passenger. There were two other guys. They were seen driving off in the Beemer. The Braintree PD's gonna have fun with this."

Jamie went silent.

"Thanks, Jamie," said Jack. "That's enough for now. You've been very helpful. Get some rest. Detective Barbado, say goodbye to the nice young man."

"Bye bye, Jamie. Have a nice life . . . in Walpole."

As they walked out, Jack pushed his hands into his coat pockets. "End of the trail for us with Jamie. He's too dumb to be connected to the massacre. He's just a punk kid jackin' cars for somebody. I guess Damone paid the price for having his Beemer in the wrong place at the wrong time."

Chapter Fifteen

On a beautiful Monday morning, Martin Douglas readied himself for work.

He was still anxious to see Maria, but calm about it this time. He thought back and realized he must have been acting like a lovesick kid. It's just as well she didn't see him like that. He probably would have scared her off.

The morning came and went. Martin taught his nine o'clock class, minus Maria Falcone. He succeeded in masking his disappointment and finished his morning in a businesslike fashion, professor mode all the way. *Go back to your office and get on with the day.* But this was unlike Maria. He hoped she was okay.

"Good morning, Mr. Douglas."

The sound of Maria's voice startled Martin, and he turned from his window, cutting off his daydream. His mouth went dry as he saw Maria standing in his office doorway. Her dark hair was pulled back and tied into a ponytail, a much different look from the elegant image he had just been viewing in dreamland. He couldn't recall seeing her look like that before, or perhaps he hadn't noticed. She was movie star material to him.

"Hello, Maria. I missed you in class this morning. Is everything all right?"

"Oh, yeah. I'm okay. I'm afraid I just got off to a late start and couldn't make it on time. I'm very sorry. It won't happen again, I promise."

Martin paused for a few seconds, catching his breath as if he had just climbed the stairs leading to his office. He gazed around his office, looking at his files and messy table. "Maria, I have something I'd like to discuss with you."

"Really. I won't miss class again, Mr. Douglas. I promise."

"No, no. It's not about that. I have—well, let's call it a business proposition for you. Maybe we could discuss it over lunch. Do you have time?"

He hoped she didn't notice the crusty remains of a sandwich on a napkin on his desk.

"Sure, I have time."

"Good. Let's go over to The Nook. My treat, if you don't object."

"That's fine."

She waited for Martin to get up from his desk. He put on the blazer he'd draped over the back of his chair and the couple wound their way through the narrow hallway around to the stairs leading to the front lobby of the building. They left the building, walked across the old covered wooden porch that ran the length of the structure and down the paved walkway toward the main street. The Nook, an old diner across the street, didn't look like much from the outside, but was a very popular eatery among the townsfolk because of its informal atmosphere and great food.

Once inside, Martin saw open seats at the counter. He looked left and right for a secluded booth instead and found one at the far end of the diner on the left. He motioned for Maria to head that way. Martin wanted to be as inconspicuous as possible. Discretion between faculty members and students wasn't always present, as Martin had heard, but it worked best for him. They walked the length of the floor and took the last booth, with Maria moving into the far seat so that she could see the entire restaurant. Martin eased himself into the near seat, his back to the establishment.

"Tell me about this business proposition, Mr. Douglas." Maria folded her hands together and rested them on the table.

"First of all, Maria, when we're away from class and other students, please call me Martin—that is, if you're comfortable with it."

Maria smiled and nodded, amused with his polite manner.

"Maria, excuse me if I'm wrong, but I get the feeling you are a little older than most of your classmates and, so, I think . . ."

"I'm twenty-four," she said, mercifully cutting him off.

Martin let out a breath as if he'd been holding one because he didn't know quite what to do with it. Relieved, he said to Maria, "Oh, that's fine. I mean, that's about what I thought. It's not that I meant to pry, of course. I was just trying to clarify things if we're going to work together."

"Are we going to work together?"

"Oh, well, that's what this meeting is about: my business proposition."

Maria was growing more amused by the moment. "Maybe you'd better tell me about that."

A waitress in a white uniform came to the booth before Martin could fumble for any more words. She engaged in the usual pleasantries and told them about the lunch specials for the day. Both agreed the New England clam chowder was a good choice on this chilly day, and they ordered it along with coffee for Martin and a Tab for Maria.

As the waitress walked away, Martin's short respite ended and he had to get back to explaining himself. He wisely decided to get right to it.

"I'm working on a book project about the New England Indians, specifically the King Phillip War in the 1670s. I've done a lot of research, but I've got a lot more to do. My papers are piling up and I could use an assistant to help me keep things organized. Just a few hours a week is all I would need. You could make your own schedule. I'll show you what to do. Everything is in my office. You could come and go as you please."

Maria listened intently to Martin's proposal and looked down at her hands. "You must really need some help with this . . . Martin."

Martin realized he had forgotten to mention that it was a paid position. "Of course, I'll pay you for the time. I didn't mean to suggest otherwise. Would three dollars an hour be okay?"

"Yeah. That's pretty good."

"Yes, well, it would only be four or five hours a week, so I was afraid you might not be interested if it was less money than that. Let's say you'll get a minimum of four hours per week, sometimes more, if needed. Would that work out for you?"

Once again the waitress interrupted the discussion as she brought the coffee and Tab to their booth. This time, it was Maria who benefited in a brief moment to contemplate this whole affair. To any other coed, three dollars an hour would be great pay. Maria found it amusing; but, of course, she couldn't let Martin know that. He seemed utterly sincere and she found him charming. This could be fun.

"Martin, could we give it a try, say for two weeks, and see how it works out? Tuesday and Thursday are best for me, since I have no afternoon classes those days. I could start tomorrow."

Martin recalled the old expression about your life flashing before your face when you are about to die. He finally relaxed, relieved that after a whole weekend of anxiety Maria gave him the positive response he had wanted.

"Yes. That makes good sense, of course. We'll try it out. That'll be fine."

"Okay. That takes care of the business part of it. Now, tell me more about the project. I think it's exciting that you're writing a book. I've never heard about the—what was it—King something War?"

"King Phillip. The King Phillip War. They don't teach about it in school. Once they get past the Pilgrims' landing and the first Thanksgiving, they jump right up to the Revolutionary War. But this was a very significant event one hundred years before the Revolution. It happened in southeastern Massachusetts. King Phillip was the son of Chief Massasoit. Phillip was his Christian name." Martin took a breath and relaxed a bit. "There's so much to catch up on, if you're interested."

"So far, I am. I'm looking forward to working on this."

"So am I. So am I."

After they finished their lunches, Martin went back to his office; Maria, to her studio apartment at Keyser Pond, driving out of town to the east up Old Concord Road to the campground and turning on to the dirt driveway entrance in front of her unit. There were two one-story buildings in an L-shaped formation of what was once a motel. Maria's unit was large enough to be comfortable for two people, with a full kitchen, bath, sleeping area and room for a sofa and easy chair. She had a small TV in one corner. The rustic atmosphere was a stark contrast to her brownstone in Boston. She could relax here. The pace was much slower. In the city, her weekends seemed to be non-stop activity. The fast pace paid off, though, into a growing bank account in New Hampshire.

Maria went into her studio apartment, dropped her bag and coat on the easy chair and kicked off her shoes. She had an hour before her late afternoon class. She looked at the bank deposit receipt from her earlier in the day. Her account balance had grown to over six figures. No wonder the bank teller gave her a funny look each time she saw Maria. But the teller never asked questions. Maria knew she'd have to move most of that money into a better place than a passbook savings account. She'd need some investing advice from a trustworthy source, someone who also did not ask questions.

On Tuesday afternoon, Maria showed up in Martin's office at two o'clock. They exchanged greetings, and Maria walked over to the table which was covered with stacks of papers and folders. "Okay, Boss. Time to tell me about this book project. Where do we begin?"

Martin, dressed in gray slacks, a long sleeved yellow shirt with a blue cardigan, was looking very much the academic type. Maria was starting to see him in a different light. She felt more relaxed in his presence. The professor-student relationship was evaporating.

"Have a seat." He motioned Maria toward the wooden armchair at the table, pulled his swivel chair out from behind his desk and moved it over beside her. "As I said yesterday, the King Phillip War was a major event in the colonial period, but it has been largely ignored in the schoolbook versions of American history. Massasoit was the chief of the Wampanoag federation when the Pilgrims arrived and settled Plymouth Colony. He maintained a fragile peace with the settlers for decades, and the Pilgrims' very survival was aided in great part by him. But, given the white man's tendency to screw up a good thing when they have the chance, they treated the Indians very badly and, over time, the relationship became hostile."

"So where did King Phillip come from?"

"He was the second son of Massasoit. His older brother was named Wamsutta. The two brothers were given English names when they were young. Wamsutta became Alexander and Pometacom became Phillip."

"PO what?"

Martin frowned at her and then smiled politely.

"His name was Pometacom, or something like that. Several spellings appear in the research. Having them take English Christian names was a political move to help in the relationship between the peoples. Alexander succeeded his father as chief. At one point, Alexander was taken into custody under suspicion of plotting a war against the English, and he died while in custody. The Indians believed he was poisoned, but there wasn't any proof. His wife, Weetamo, led the people for a while and was known as the Squaw Sachem. Phillip eventually became the federation leader and after the war was underway, Weetamo died of drowning while trying to escape an English military attack. At least that appears to have been the case. Her body was recovered and her head was cut off and impaled on a pole and put up in public in the Taunton area."

"Too bad. Sounds like she was a tough woman."

"Yes, I'd say she was. But sometimes being tough doesn't ensure survival."

Maria stared intensely at Martin, drinking in his words.

Maria's love of history began to play on her. "This sounds like a fascinating story. I'm getting interested already. It'll be fun to learn about an historical event without having to take any tests or write papers."

She suddenly felt a little embarrassed, fearing she had said something disrespectful of Martin's profession. "No offense, of course."

"None taken."

Martin showed Maria his files and sought her ideas on how best to organize them. Martin made a good effort at using a chronological system, and he date stamped each paper in the margin. But he had no efficient cross-reference, so Maria went to work photocopying everything and setting up a cross-reference system. She also went about creating an index. The more she worked at it, the more she realized the job could be bigger than Martin had estimated.

Maria enjoyed the work with Martin, and she especially enjoyed the solitude of his office. The entire Inn was a relatively quiet building, even though it was full of faculty department offices, the college business office, the registrar's office and a mail room in the basement. The old colonial design provided for a great deal of isolation and privacy, which served its original guests very well. It didn't bother the current occupants, either. Maria found it a stark contrast to her life in Boston.

Before the trial period was up, Maria knew that she'd keep the part time job. To her, it was a much better way of spending her spare time than watching soccer games or drinking at The Pub. Sue, however, was growing concerned. How could Maria do this? She was spending even more time away from the college life that most kids enjoyed. Why work at a dull job in an instructor's office? Could she have some interest in Mr. Douglas?

One afternoon while working in Martin's office, Sue stopped by and saw Martin seated at his desk talking to Maria.

"Excuse me, Mr. Douglas, I was looking for Maria, but I shouldn't interrupt you while you're working." Sue spoke rapidly. Maria's head spun around at the sound of her voice.

"Hello, Sue," said Martin. "No problem. In fact, I need to be going anyway. You kids feel free to stay and chat. Maria, you can close up when you leave."

Maria nodded, looking a bit surprised and annoyed at Sue's appearance. Martin grabbed some papers, stashed them into his bag which he slung over his shoulder while getting up. He slid out from behind his desk, bid goodbye to the young women and hustled down the back stairs of The Inn, like he was late for an appointment.

Sue grinned sheepishly at Martin's nervous behavior, but her expression changed quickly to a more serious look when Maria spoke.

"What are you doing here, Sue?"

"I'm sorry, Maria. I've hardly seen you for the last couple of weeks, so I just thought I might try to catch you here to see what's going on, that's all."

"What's going on? What did you think was going on? I told you about this job with Martin, ah, Mr. Douglas. There's no mystery here."

Sue could see this talk escalating into an argument and she tried to defuse it. "All right. That came out wrong. I'm sorry. It's just that, well, you're all about work; school work, your weekend job, now this. And, pardon me, maybe it's just a job to you but I think Mr. Douglas has a pretty strong gleam in his eye when he looks at you. Not that there's anything wrong with that, mind you. I just happened to notice, that's all."

Maria took a deep breath and let it out slowly. "Yes, I think he's interested in me, but if he is, he's awfully slow in getting around to things. I've been working for him for two weeks and he hasn't asked me out to anything more than lunch."

Sue's eyes widened. "If he did ask you out, would you say yes?"

"Possibly. You know that I'm not interested in any college guys. Mr. Douglas is much more my type. No offense toward Dean, but—well, you know what I mean."

Sue looked at Maria indicating that she didn't really know what she meant at all. Maria paused, seeing by Sue's expression that her last remark didn't help.

"Look, I'm twenty-four years old, so I'm not that much younger than Martin. If he's about thirty and I'm twenty-four, what's wrong with that?" Sue had never known Maria's exact age before and seemed a little stunned. To a twenty-one-year-old college senior, a fellow student who was twenty-four seemed a bit old. Her perspective changed.

Sue looked out into the hallway and then closed the door to the office and stepped toward Maria. "You know, maybe you're right. Maybe going out with a faculty member could be kind of cool." Sue sat on top of a corner of the table facing Maria and became energized. "There's nothing wrong with that. It's not like you're an underclassman, you know, some teeny bopper who's all starry eyed over a prof. You should definitely go out with him if he asks."

Maria thought perhaps she'd let her guard down for a moment and spoken too much about herself. That was uncharacteristic. In her mind, she was momentarily comparing Martin to Ben Secani and her customers in Boston. It was charming how Martin stumbled for words and was nervous when alone with her. But she mustn't reveal any of this to Sue. She composed herself and spoke calmly. "I don't know if there's anything cool about it. He's just a nice guy who's taken an interest in me. But he hasn't even asked me out yet."

"Yeah, but he will." Sue poked her finger at Maria as if to say just wait and see. "He's single, new guy in town . . . got to be horny." Both women laughed at the assessment. "Before long, you might be screwing a prof!"

Maria had been thinking of asking Sue to go to the Pub for a glass of wine, but decided against it. She didn't want Sue to take this *screwing a prof* thing any further, certainly not in a public place. She smiled at Sue and went back to filing some papers. Sue got the message.

"Well, I guess you've got to earn your keep. I'll let you get back to work. See you at dinner?"

"Yeah. See you in the cafeteria."

Sue headed toward the door, opened it and stepped halfway through. Then she turned quickly and said, "Leave some perfume on his desk. Keep him hot!"

Maria shook her head and waved Sue out the door with a smile. The *keep him hot* expression stuck with her. Imagine, a guy actually liking her; not just horny or wanting to show off a beautiful young escort to the rich and powerful. But look where it got Dad with Mom. *Be careful,* she thought. *Be careful.*

Chapter Sixteen

Jimmy was packed with nervous energy waiting for his friend to arrive. He'd been working on this plan for weeks, and it was time to get it going. He had to field his team, one that could help him build his reputation.

When Johnny arrived, Jimmy gave him a hand slap and his friend took a seat. Jimmy grabbed two beers from his fridge, opened both and handed one to his buddy sitting in the lone easy chair in the one-room flat. Jimmy paced the floor, too excited to sit. They took a couple of swallows.

"Are you sure we can do this, Jimmy?"

"I'm positive. I've checked this place out, and it'll be a snap."

"It better be."

"What the hell, you gettin' nervous, Johnny?"

"Don't get me wrong. I'm cool with the idea. It's just we never did anything like this before. We gotta make sure we got all the bases covered. Ya know what I mean."

"Don't worry. I'm tellin' ya, I've checked it all out. We just need one more guy. I'll handle the wheels. You and him make the hit. Talk to Frankie."

"I already gave him the word about a possible job, somethin' big time. He likes it. He just needs the details, that's all. He'll be ready to go."

"Johnny, this is gonna be so cool. Secani thinks I'm just good for small time stuff, but this'll show him he's been wrong about me. After this job, he's gonna give me more important stuff."

"What kinda jobs do you think we'll get? I heard he's just a hit man."

"Oh, no, man. He's higher up than that. He won't tell me directly, but I know he does other things. He hangs out a lot at Club 77, so I figure he's tight with the guys there . . . probably the boss man, Joe Vito."

"Joe Vito. If Secani's in with him, that's real big time. Yeah, this should really make you with Secani. What about me and Frankie? We gonna fit into your big plans after?"

"Of course, Johnny. You guys'll be my team. Secani'll see I can do bigger jobs 'cause it's not just me. I'll have my own guys. He'll see we can do all kinds of work. I'm tellin' ya, John, he's gonna love this. Look, it'll make him look great, too. His boss'll see Secani is stronger and probably promote him, or somethin' like that. We make more money, Secani makes more, and so does his boss. That's the way it goes. Hey, he may even let me take a tumble with that sweet piece of his in the Back Bay. I'm getting' a hard on just thinkin' about it."

"Yeah, man. Maybe I can get a turn, too. I'll take sloppy seconds."

"Don't push it, pal. Secani keeps her on a short leash. You'll get somethin' all right. They got some hot dancers in the Zone. I'll see what I can do for ya."

Johnny got up from his chair and strutted up to Jimmy. They clinked their beers together. "I'm really startin' to like the sound of this whole move, Jimmy boy."

"Me, too. And this is just the beginnin.' We're gonna have dough up the yingy, broads all over the place and a solid spot in the organization. Ya know, I was getting' pretty pissed at Secani, the way he treats me sometimes. Now it's gonna change, buddy. We're gonna show 'em all. We're gonna move up."

"More dough sounds real good, Jimmy. I lost a few at a poker game the other night. I can use the bucks."

"Oh, one more thing. If we gotta take somebody out, you good with that?"

"Ah, yeah, I'm good. I mean, I ain't done it yet, but I wanna get one under my belt, ya know."

"That's the way I figure it, too, and I got the hardware. Good stuff."

The two men chugged down the beers. Johnny almost choked on his and ran to the sink to spit it out. Jimmy laughed hard. When he caught his breath, Johnny laughed, too.

"Well, you better try that again," said Jimmy, as he fetched more beer. "Let the celebration go on. This'll be a night to remember."

Chapter Seventeen

The Tufts University campus sits on a hill in Medford about five or six miles out of Boston to the northwest. In a rectangular configuration of buildings atop the hill, a two-story brick colonial building houses the bookstore. On the second floor, a counter divides the stacks of books and a cash register kiosk from the business area with its gray metal desks and an inner office for the store manager. He was replying to a phone call.

"Yes, we have a deposit ready to go. Thanks." Walt Zimmerman hung up the phone, walked out of his office and stood facing the young man and two women at their desks comprising the rest of the bookstore's full-time staff. He had a heavy satchel in one hand. "Stan, the deposit is ready to go. The Security escort will be here in a minute."

Stan Moore, his twenty-five-year-old assistant manager, had begun to get up from his chair before Walt had started to speak, He knew the drill.

Stan had worked at the bookstore for four years and had become the assistant manager after the woman who'd held the position previously retired six months earlier. She used to make up the deposits, and Walt rode to the bank with the Security guard, but now Stan got to ride shotgun after Walt made up the deposit. It was not a duty he cherished. Stan took the satchel from Walt and brought it back to his desk while he put on his light jacket.

Soon Joe LaLiberty, a husky man in a blue Security uniform arrived and stood at the counter, resting his elbows on it and smiling at the staff. "Good afternoon, folks."

"Hi, Joe. Let's rock and roll." He grabbed the satchel and followed the armed guard down the stairs, out of the rear door to the building and into the Ford Crown Victoria marked with Tufts Security on the sides and blue lights on the roof.

The Crown Vic turned left out of the parking lot and then took a series of left turns as it wound down the hill and eventually reached College Avenue, a route that put them on the right side of the road and at the curb outside the M&S Bank at the turn where College Avenue meets Boston Avenue. A dark green Chevrolet Impala was parked a car's length ahead of them where the red paint clearly said *Fire Lane—No Parking.*

"That's cute," said Joe. "Wait here a minute."

"Okay. No rush."

Just as Joe pushed the gear lever on the steering column up into the Park position and put on the emergency brake, two men came running out of the bank, pushing a couple of pedestrians aside. One man held a money bag in each hand. The other held one money bag in his left hand and a gun in his right. He instinctively fired a shot at the Crown Vic, with its police car look, piercing the windshield cleanly in the center.

"Get down," shouted Joe as both men slouched in the front seat, getting as low as they could and ducking the flying windshield glass. A third man was behind the wheel of the green car, keeping the motor running. He sped off down Boston Avenue as soon as his partners were inside the doors, one man in the front passenger seat and the other in back. Joe sat up as he heard the Impala take off, quickly put the Crown Vic in gear and gave chase after grabbing his car radio microphone with his free hand. "Car three to base. There's a bank robbery in progress. Shots fired at me. I'm in pursuit northbound on Boston Ave." Joe turned on his siren and lights.

"You okay, Stan?"

"Yeah. Nothing that a change of underwear won't fix."

Jimmy *Slick* Morelli was checking his rearview mirror for the Crown Vic and didn't notice Audrey Green, a beautiful twenty-one-year-old female student, clutching her books in front of her and crossing Boston Avenue. It was too late. The Impala hit her and sent her up onto the hood and over the roof. She landed with a dull thud on the street behind the speeding car. She was dead before hitting the ground.

"Aw, shit!" screamed Jimmy. He looked back in his rearview mirror and his car began to swerve on Boston Avenue.

"Watch what you're doing," yelled his partner beside him. Johnny tried to grab the steering wheel, but Jimmy slapped at his hands.

"Get your freakin' hands off the wheel." Jimmy was starting to panic.

The brief argument with Johnny caused Jimmy to lose control of the Impala. It failed to follow the curve in the road to the left and shot up over a short embankment. Jimmy hit the brakes and tried to steer the car away from the trees ahead of it, to no avail. The Impala slowed somewhat, but couldn't stop in time to avoid hitting a large oak head-on. The driver and his passengers were thrown forward with a jolt. Jimmy's chest hit the steering column hard before he continued upward, his head going into the windshield. Johnny crashed into the dashboard before he, too, struck the windshield. Both men were knocked out cold. The man in the rear flew over the seat backs and slammed into the men in front of him. He remained conscious, but stunned. Soon he would feel the pain of his broken collarbone.

As the Crown Vic approached, Joe hit the brakes and turned his car to the right side of the road, stopping before reaching Audrey's lifeless body. "Oh, my God!" he moaned, his breath short and his heart pounding.

Both men got out of the car. Stan tried to catch his breath, feeling as if a flailing aircraft he was riding in had just made an emergency landing. His face showed his horror.

"Oh, geeze," he cried. "I know that girl. She works in the bookstore, on work-study." He stood there shaking his head.

Joe rushed to his car radio and called for an ambulance while Stan stood by Audrey and waved traffic away. Approaching cars slowed down and stopped. A security guard from the bank came running down the street and helped Joe redirect traffic. Within a couple of minutes, other Tufts Security cars arrived on the scene. Joe gave a quick description of the Impala to one of the drivers and he took off in the direction of the robbers, his siren blaring and lights flashing. He only needed a few seconds to reach the curve where the Impala went off the road.

Chapter Eighteen

Within an hour, Jack Contino heard about the attempted bank robbery on the Tufts campus. Being a resident of Somerville, this news got his attention since it was just a few miles away from his home. Jack was on the phone to the Medford PD seconds after he got the story. He had a young son who often played with buddies in a ball field not far from the small branch of the M&S Bank. When he heard about the coed being struck and killed by the speeding getaway car, it gave the big man a chill.

"Where'd they take them?" Jack demanded over the phone. "Okay. Thanks," he said and hung up. Leo Barbado watched from his desk as Jack concluded his phone call.

"They took the bastards to Mass General so they can hold them at Charles Street overnight," Jack announced. "The wheel man was a guy named Jimmy Morelli. Charlie mentioned him before. He works the streets a lot, but Charlie never said who he works for."

"Yeah. He's a punk kid who's done some short time starting in juvenile. He's a regular in the Zone. He's a small timer, never bank robbery."

"Well, he's in it big this time, robbing a bank and killing that girl. The punks got banged up a bit. Too bad. They probably won't get out of the trauma unit for a while. Let's give them an hour and then go pay them a visit. I have a feeling Agent Nelson is going to be calling us about this one."

Massachusetts General Hospital is a short walk from the old Charles Street Jail, one of the most famous landmarks in Boston. Built in 1851, it housed many notable prisoners over the years, including James Michael Curley, the former mayor of the city; and Sacco and Vanzetti, the anarchists convicted of armed robbery and murder in Braintree, Massachusetts in 1920. One of the top hospitals in the country, Mass General had treated many wealthy people. Celebrities had gone there for treatment of various ills. This day it accepted for admittance three men: killers and bank robbers.

Jack and Leo identified themselves at the front desk of the hospital and were directed to a room down one level. As they got off the elevator, they looked both ways, searching for room B122. It didn't matter. Jack saw two State Police Troopers four rooms down to his left and headed in that direction. The troopers were tall and wore the blue uniforms, riding britches and high leather boots, indicative of the Motorcycle Unit of the Field Services—Tactical Operations. The unit served a variety of special assignments from escorting VIPs to guarding prisoners.

Jack and Leo held out their badges as they approached the troopers. One of them stepped forward. "Are you attached to the FBI? We were told that some MET cops working with the Bureau would be coming."

Jack looked at Leo. "I told you we'd be hearing from Agent Nelson."

The State Trooper nodded when he heard Nelson's name.

"Where's Morelli?" Jack asked.

The trooper pointed to the room where Jimmy lay in bed, awake but groggy from the ordeal.

"The others are in the two rooms across the hall."

Jack and Leo looked at each other and then back at the troopers.

"We'll talk to Morelli," said Jack. The trooper stepped aside.

Jimmy Morelli lay in his bed looking like a guy who'd just made a big mistake with a motor vehicle. His eyes were closed, his head showed black and blue marks and some dried blood on his scalp.

"Open your eyes, Jimmy," said Leo. "We know you're awake. It's time for a chat."

Jimmy opened his eyes slowly, his face twisted in a grimace. "Who the hell are you?"

"Detectives Contino and Barbado, Metropolitan District Commission Police attached to the Federal Bureau of Investigation, at your service," answered Jack. "You're in a lot of trouble, Jimmy boy."

Morelli's face turned to a look of fear and he closed his eyes again.

Jack pulled a metal chair close to the bed and sat on it facing the backrest, his arms crossed over the top. He spoke softly. "You've got a lot of problems, Jimmy. First, it's against the law to rob banks. And it's not nice to shoot at anybody, let alone a security guard. But here's the kicker, Jimmy, and this is the worst of it. That girl you hit with your car is dead. We're going to see if a murder charge will fit you, Jimmy."

"Hey, that was an accident. She ran out into traffic. I couldn't help that. I didn't mean to kill anybody."

"Tell that to her family," snapped Jack.

Jimmy started to tremble.

Jack got up from his chair and pushed it aside. He stood beside the bed, forcing Morelli to look up at him. "Tell me, Jimmy: what on earth were you guys doing trying to rob that little bank? That's not in your league. Obviously, you're not any good at it and now you've got enough charges against you to give you a permanent new address in Walpole. Who put you up to this, Jimmy?"

"Nobody put me up to it. Hey, this was my own gig. I needed to make some big money. I needed to show Secani that I could . . ."

Jimmy's voice trailed off as he realized that he'd blurted out his boss's name. Jack looked over at Leo, recognizing the name he'd found written in Tom Jacobs' notepad. Jack turned back to Morelli.

"Who's that, Jimmy?" asked Jack. Jimmy averted his eyes from the cops. Jack asked again. "Who's Secani, Jimmy?" Jimmy was silent.

Jack walked back to Leo and grinned slightly like a man who'd just been dealt a good poker hand. "You know, I think we need to let Jimmy rest and collect his thoughts." Leo nodded.

"Jimmy," Jack continued, "they're going to move you over to Charles Street pretty soon. Get a good rest. We'll come back to chat again soon. Be thinking about that new address I said you're going to have."

Jack and Leo left the room and bid farewell to the troopers standing guard. Jimmy Morelli lay on his bed and started to sob.

The morning after visiting Jimmy, Jack and Leo were at the Charles Street Jail at about 10:00 a.m. Entering the rotunda with its high atrium and identifying themselves to the officer on duty at the visitor's area, they were then taken to a section of the jail that showed the old original brick walls. The visiting rooms had been updated with modern security devices and electronic surveillance. Their shoes made loud claps as they walked across the old floor beneath the ceiling. They passed through a large room with Plexiglas windows separating the visitors from the prisoners and were taken into a smaller room with a table, four chairs and no windows. The larger room was for the general public who came to visit family members, friends, colleagues and, sometimes, enemies who were prisoners. The smaller room was for police interrogation.

A young man in a cast and sling wearing an orange jumpsuit was brought in, escorted by two large guards. He complied with their command to sit at the table.

"All yours, gentlemen," said one of the guards as they left the room.

John Gangi, Morelli's gunman, was a baby-faced twenty-five-year-old with dark hair and bushy eyebrows, under six feet tall with a stocky build.

Leo stayed on his feet while Jack sat at the table across from Gangi. "You're in a lot of trouble, John," said Jack. "Good thing for you you're a lousy shot. It could be worse. If you'd hit that Security guard or his passenger, you might be up for murder one. As it is, you do have that young woman's death on your hands. No telling what the D.A. will do with that. You might not be clear of a murder charge after all."

Gangi sat still, keeping his eyes looking down, playing the stoic tough guy. Jack expected that.

Leo paced the floor, just to get Gangi's attention. Jack stared straight ahead at him, watching his expression. When he saw a nervous reaction to Leo, Jack spoke again.

"Your record is pretty light, up to now; but this is big, John. You could be looking at some real hard time."

"No juvenile hall this time," said Leo. "No Concord. This time it's Walpole. It's hard there, John. There are lifers there who like to dominate young guys like you. Some of them like to get real cozy."

Gangi started to twitch.

Jack leaned in toward the prisoner and spoke softly, but firmly. "This is no time to play the tough guy. Your only hope is to cooperate with us. You don't want to spend the rest of your life in prison, John. If you help us, we might be able to help you. Talk to us about this bank job, John. Who put you up to it and why?"

Gangi began to move nervously in his seat as the words began to sink in. Finally, he spoke in a high pitched voice that contrasted with his tough-looking build.

"Morelli. It was his idea. He said it would be a cinch. We'd make a big score and the bosses would be impressed."

"The bosses?" queried Jack. "Who are the bosses?"

Gangi became more agitated. "I don't know. Morelli said he works for a guy who's connected, you know—the Mafia or something."

"Has this guy got a name?" asked Jack.

"Morelli calls him Ben, that's all. I don't know his last name."

"Wait a minute," said Leo. "A lightweight like Jimmy Morelli is the brains behind a bank job?"

"Yeah. That's right. Like I said, Jimmy came to me about it. He said it would be an easy score, being a small bank like that. He was tired of being treated like a minor league guy. He said this would be our chance. He said we needed one more guy, so I got my cousin, Frankie, to join us. By the way, how is he, Frankie?"

"He's okay," said Leo. "He's a little busted up, but he'll be all right. We'll tell him you were concerned when we see him." He grinned at Jack.

Jack wanted to get back to Secani. "Do you know anything else about Secani?"

"No, not really," he answered. "Jimmy says he works for him, but he didn't tell me what he actually does." Gangi paused as if he was scanning his brain for something to offer. He was afraid that he didn't know enough of value to tell the cops. He needed a way to help himself. "Jimmy . . ." Gangi started to speak and then stopped. "Jimmy says that Ben's got a girl who does tricks for him and they're pretty close. He says she's prime stuff, you know, and how he'd like to get some time with her, but Ben wouldn't let him. I don't know her name or anything." Jack looked up at Leo. They were getting somewhere.

Jack motioned to his partner, who nodded back at him and then opened the door and called the guard. John Gangi was helped up from his chair and taken out of the room.

"We need to have more chats like this, John," said Jack as the prisoner was taken away. "They're good for you."

Leo moved closer to Jack and spoke in a near whisper. "What do you think, partner?"

"I think we know some things we didn't two days ago. We now have Secani's first name: Ben, and we have a possible chink in his armor: a girl who does tricks for him and gives Morelli a tilt in his kilt. Let's get him in here."

Within a few minutes, Jack and Leo were continuing their interrogation, only this time with Jimmy Morelli. "You look better after a night's rest and some cleaning up," said Leo. "But you don't look much like a tough bank robber. We understand that Secani has a hooker under his wing who's top shelf."

Jimmy looked surprised. "Who's been talking to you, Gangi? Don't believe anything he says. He'll lie through his teeth."

"Look, Jimmy," said Leo. "Somebody's going to fall hard in this because of the dead college girl, and Gangi doesn't want to be the one. If he helps us out, then where will that leave you? There's only so much room in the life boat."

"Like I said, he'll make up anything to save himself."

"Aw, come on. He's too dumb to make this up and you know it. Tell us about Secani's girl. Do you know where she lives? What's her name?"

Jimmy Morelli was at a fork in the road of his life's journey. If he cooperated with the cops, his life would be in danger from Ben Secani. If he stonewalled it, he could wind up in prison for the rest of his life, where he'd be low on the pecking order. Bad things happen in prison. At least the cops might be able to hide him. "She lives in the Back Bay, on Marlborough Street, I think. I had to take Ben there once when his car was in the shop. I don't remember the address," said Jimmy, having decided which fork in the road to take. "He called her Maria. I never heard her last name."

Jack wrote this down as Leo continued his questioning. "Have you ever seen her?"

Jimmy nodded.

"Describe her for us, Jimmy."

"She's about five-foot-three, compact build, you know . . . she's got all the stuff in the right places, really fills out a sweater. She's got black hair and blue eyes, beautiful. Too bad Ben keeps her out of reach."

Jack stood up from his chair and put his notepad away. "Jimmy, how'd you like to get some fresh air?"

"What do you mean?"

"Maybe you don't remember the address but I'll bet you remember the building," said Jack. "Perhaps you could show it to us. We could arrange for you to take a little ride with us. What do you say?"

Jack drove while Leo and Jimmy sat in the backseat. Jimmy was in a dark trench coat to hide his orange jumpsuit and handcuffs. They headed down Storrow Drive and took the Massachusetts Avenue exit, then headed back up Marlborough Street. Jack slowed down to a crawl while Jimmy looked for a familiar building. They crossed the intersection at Hereford Street and then Gloucester. Just before they reached Fairfield Street Jimmy called out.

"That one, the brownstone on the right. I think that was it."

Jack pulled up to the next open space along the curb, not far up the road.

"I'll go check it out," said Jack, stepping out of the car and walking quickly back to the building. The large detective walked up the stairs that led to the outside doorway and went in. He checked all the mailboxes of the three story building and found one possibility, an M. Falcone on the third floor. He rang the buzzer, but there was no answer. He tried it a second time with the same result.

"Nobody home," he said, as he climbed back into the driver's seat. He turned to face his backseat riders. "There's an M. Falcone on the third floor. Does that sound familiar, Jimmy?"

"Like I said, I don't remember ever hearing Ben say her last name. The M, though, that could be it, you know, Maria. I never went in. I just saw her come out with Ben once."

Jack wrote the address in his notepad. "Okay. We'll have to come back later when we won't be imposing on Mr. Morelli's time."

The detectives took Jimmy back to the Charles Street Jail. "You think he was just taking us for a joyride, Jack?" asked Leo.

"I'm not sure. I don't think so. Won't be hard to find out. Let's swing by the Registry of Deeds and see who owns that building. Then we can get the full name of M. Falcone on the third floor."

The search told them the building on Marlborough Street was owned by Lane Realty, a company that owned several apartment buildings in Boston. The detectives went to the main office on Commonwealth Avenue, just a couple of blocks away from the address in question. The receptionist was about to tell them that Mr. Lane was not available when Jack and Leo produced their police identification. Suddenly, Mr. Lane was available.

Mr. Lane was a short, balding man in his fifties. He dressed the role of the business leader with a blue business suit, suspenders and a red tie over a long sleeve white dress shirt. "What can I do for you gentlemen?"

"We'd like to know the name of a tenant of yours at this address," said Jack as he slipped Mr. Lane a piece of paper.

"Certainly. Oh, Miss Salisbury, get the name of the tenant at this address," he said, passing the paper to his receptionist. "Is there anything wrong, detectives?"

"I hope not," said Jack. "We're just interested in the occupant there, that's all."

The receptionist returned with a file folder. "That apartment," she said, reading from the file inside, "is rented by a Mr. Benjamin Secani. The rent is paid in full. He's been renting there for six years. No problems and no complaints of any kind."

"Sounds like a peach of a tenant," said Leo.

"Thank you, Mr. Lane," said Jack. "That's all we needed to know. We appreciate your cooperation." Jack and Leo nodded to Miss Salisbury and walked back to their car.

Once on the sidewalk, Jack turned to Leo. "Well, that's our boy, Ben Secani. Seems like a perfect tenant, except that he's not the tenant. And M. Falcone must be our girl, Maria."

"If she turns tricks at that apartment, maybe we should stake it out and go for a bust," said Leo.

"No, I don't think so. If she's as hot a number as Morelli says, she's probably a high class call girl, strictly outcall. We've got to go slowly here. Secani is connected to the North End massacre, somehow. Morelli works for him, but tried the bank on his own volition. Remember what Agent Nelson said, see how things play. We've got to smoke him out. Maybe we can do that through Maria Falcone."

"Yeah, that makes sense. Your lead, Detective."

Later that day Jack got on the phone with Agent Nelson and brought him up to date on his progress. Nelson was pleased to hear about the lead and promised the FBI would run a check on Secani. It's funny, Jack thought, how things sometimes work out in a case. Secani's name is in a notebook belonging to one of the shooting victims, but he's an unknown. Then some schmuck tries to pull off a bank robbery, screws it up and blabs Secani's name while being interrogated. Bank robber schmuck number two gives us his first name and, voila, we have Ben Secani, a real person. This real person has a broad named Maria Falcone who lives in an apartment paid for by Secani. Soon they'd meet this girl in the flesh, so to speak, and they'd learn more about Secani through her. They were making some headway.

Chapter Nineteen

Where Jimmy Morelli felt fear, Joe Vito showed anger. The news of the attempted bank robbery didn't sit well with him. Seated at his office desk at Club 77, he poured two bourbons and slid one across the desk toward Ben Secani.

"I know you didn't put Morelli and those two punks up to this, but tell me: what the hell was he thinking?" Joe's voice could best be described as highly irritated. "Robbing a freakin' bank! Who the hell does he think he is, Jesse James? Jesus Christ! What a stupid damn thing to do! This is the kind of dumb stunt that would have driven Gus absolutely crazy, may he rest in peace."

Gus *The Boat* Botelli, had passed away two years ago from natural causes. Of course, in his line of work, natural causes could mean a bullet in the skull, but Gus died of an aggressive brain cancer. Ben nodded as he sipped his drink.

Joe was concerned that a member of the organization was in FBI custody under heavy guard. This sent a signal through the law enforcement agencies that opened an opportunity for deal making. It could draw unwarranted attention from a low level gang member. As far as the cops were concerned, it was the start of fishing season.

"Jimmy's got nothing to give them," assured Ben. "He does some collection work for me and some street hustling. He seems a little ambitious sometimes and he wants to impress me, hoping he can move up in the organization, but he doesn't have the brains for it."

"How about the other two?"

"I don't know them. Must be friends of Jimmy's. I'll check on them. Should I prepare for action?"

"No. We'd better not try to move on them. That would just convince the cops these guys were worth something. Besides, with the FBI looking into a bank robbery, they'll be under heavy guard. The public is going to be pissed about that girl getting killed, which means the politicians are going to want to give them a scapegoat. We'd better stay clear of those idiots, at least for now. Once they're in Walpole, the situation might change for them."

Ben drank more bourbon, maintaining his cool for Joe. Although Joe had assessed the situation pretty well, Ben didn't like feeling vulnerable, and his connection to Jimmy Morelli made him feel that way. Gus had always taught him to cover his tracks, which he had with success during his career. But he had no way of anticipating this grandstand move by Jimmy. Joe said not to move, so he wouldn't—but deep inside he wanted to clean up the situation as soon as possible. He didn't want any police attention to drift his way.

"Joe, you just said it was fishing season. Maybe that's the answer. Maybe we can throw them a fish, like a red herring."

Joe gave Ben a quizzical look. "I don't follow."

Ben answered carefully. "Maybe we can set up a decoy, make it look like Jimmy's got a connection that goes nowhere, or goes to Bellino."

Joe was skeptical. "Ah, I don't know, Ben. That might get complicated and could backfire on us. Screwing Bellino would be fun, but he'll be pissed that it happened in his territory. I'll have to cool him off. Like I said before, let's just steer clear for now."

"Okay, but let me think about it. Maybe I can come up with a good plan that might change your mind."

"Okay. You go *think* about it, but don't make any moves."

Chapter Twenty

Maria had started putting papers away and straightening up the work area in Martin's office after Sue left, when she heard Martin's voice at the door.

"Excuse me, Maria. I hope I didn't startle you."

"No, you didn't, but I thought you were gone for the night," said Maria, a slight sound of suspicion in her voice.

"Well, I was talking to some folks in the Business Office, so I never really left the building. I decided to take a chance you might still be here. I wanted to ask you something." Maria seemed to accept the explanation and Martin relaxed.

"What's that, Martin?" asked Maria as she resumed her cleanup activities, not looking up.

Martin felt his mouth becoming dry and he struggled to get the question out, knowing that there was no turning back now. "I was wondering, Maria, if you'd like to have dinner with me tonight."

Maria stopped what she was doing and looked straight at Martin. Slowly, a smile began to appear on her face, but before she could say anything, Martin spoke again.

"You've been doing great work here and I thought it would be nice if we could have a casual dinner together, sort of a reward."

Maria's smile went away and she walked up to Martin, standing close.

"Is that why you want to have dinner with me, Martin, to reward me for my work?"

Martin paused before answering, realizing he should be more direct with her. "Well, no, not entirely. I want to have dinner with you because . . . I want to spend time with you away from my office and my classroom."

Maria smiled again.

"That's better, Martin," she said. "Do you know where Keyser Pond Campground is?"

Martin nodded.

"I'm in unit four. I park my hatchback right in front. What time can I expect you?"

"I'll pick you up at six."

The two smiled at each other and Martin turned to leave the room, a feeling of ease coming over him. At that moment, Maria was no longer just a student. She was a new woman in his life for whom he held great interest.

Before going back to her apartment, Maria decided to swing by Sue's place to tell her about her new dinner plans. She knocked on the door and waited briefly before Sue opened it and motioned Maria inside.

"I can't stay long, but I thought I should tell you that my dinner plans have changed. Now, don't get pissed at me, but I'm going out with Martin."

Sue's eyes widened and she laughed out loud.

"Well that sure was fast. Where did that come from?"

"Martin came back to the office after you left and he asked me to go out with him tonight."

"Do you think he was waiting for me to leave? I'll bet he was!"

"He said he was in the Business Office and he decided to take a chance I'd still be there," continued Maria. "I don't know. He doesn't strike me as the impulsive type, so I think he's been working on this for a while. At any rate, I just thought I should let you know that I won't be in the dining hall tonight."

Sue grabbed Maria and gave her a hug. "Well, you go out and have yourself a great time!"

Maria stiffened at the surprise hug and smiled. "Thanks. I will. Talk to you later."

Maria shook her head as she walked back to her car. Sue seemed more excited about this date than she was. Then she realized that from Sue's perspective, Maria never had dates. She didn't know the half.

The weather was cooperative and a predicted rain was holding off until later in the evening. Martin grabbed a tan trench coat as he left his house wearing brown slacks and a green pullover sweater. No sport coat tonight. He wanted a more casual look. He hopped into his Jeep, started the engine and headed to Maria's apartment.

Maria's clothes closet in Henniker was far simpler than the one in Boston. She had little need for expensive looking outfits here, but she managed to keep a few nice ones on hand, just in case. For tonight she selected a red pants suit and a black blouse. The pants fit quite snuggly so she decided to keep the jacket off until Martin had a chance to see her figure. She was actually looking forward to this date for personal enjoyment. What a twist! Maria combed her long, dark hair and sat on her small sofa, listening to the college radio station while waiting.

The headlights from Martin's Jeep flashed quickly through the partially opened drapes of Maria's apartment and signaled his arrival. She heard his door close as he exited his Jeep and walked to her apartment door, where he knocked quickly three times. When she appeared in the open doorway, Martin saw someone other than the Maria he had been talking to before. Here was a beautiful young woman, poised and enticing in her red suit. She welcomed him in and turned to walk toward her suit jacket draped over a chair. This was a choreographed move, planned to get Martin's attention. It did that.

"You look terrific," said Martin. Those were all the words he needed to say. His face said the rest. Maria smiled and thanked him as she slipped on the jacket and loosely tied the sash around her waist. Her full breasts were very evident, and her entire figure was now on display, much to Martin's satisfaction.

"Where are we going tonight?" asked Maria, breaking Martin's concentration on his date's figure.

"Do you like Japanese food? There's a good Japanese restaurant in Concord where they cook the food at your table."

"That sounds like fun. Let's go."

The date was off to a good start, as Martin saw it. Although he expected more casual dress from Maria, he was ecstatic about her choice of clothes and he thought a Japanese restaurant would add a novel touch to the event. He wished he was putting her into a limo instead of his Jeep.

The ride went quickly as they had some polite conversation and soon were headed north on Main Street in Concord. Martin turned into the restaurant's parking lot and was able to park close to the door. He held his trench coat noticed that Maria hadn't brought one, as if she was immune to foul weather when she looked so stunning.

The hostess seated them quickly at a table already occupied by two other couples. The table wrapped around a large steel grill on three sides. The fourth side left room for the cook and his utensils. A waitress came around and took drink orders. At Martin's recommendation, they ordered two Black Belts, a version of a Black Russian, only Saki was used in place of vodka with the Kahlua. The couple looked over their menus while waiting for their drinks.

"What do you recommend?" asked Maria. "I gather you've been here before."

"Yes, I have. What I like is that I can stick to foods I normally have, like steak or seafood, but the preparation and seasoning will give it the Asian flair. And you're going to like the show."

"The show?"

"The cook entertains a little at each table. You'll see. I think I'll go with the shrimp flambé appetizer and a filet mignon, medium rare."

"Well, I'll make it easy for the waiter and order the same," said Maria, smiling. "So he's going to light up the place?"

"For a second or two. You'll see. Watch your eyebrows!"

After the waitress brought their drinks, she also took everyone's orders at the table. Martin raised his glass and made a toast to his date. "To our first dinner together . . . and to the project, of course."

"Of course." She took a sip of her Black Belt. "Oh, that's good."

Martin grinned. Maria was showing very positive signs. He hadn't had good female companionship in a long time.

Martin looked over at Maria, as if to say now watch this. The chef appeared, greeted the guests at the table and began his work. He fired up his grill and then arranged his utensils while the grill reached high heat. He took out a plastic bottle of cooking oil and spread a stream of oil across the grill while squeezing a friction lighter with the other. A second later a high flame rose up, running across the grill.

"Whew!" exclaimed Maria, grabbing Martin's left forearm with her right hand. "You can really feel that heat!"

Martin smiled as he glanced at her hand on his arm. *Contact!*

The chef had a tray brought out to him that contained all the foods he was to cook for the customers at his table. A large batch of fried rice went on to a section of the grill, and he spread it around with two spatulas, occasionally tapping them on the edge of the grill. Then he dropped some shrimp onto the grill in front of Maria and Martin. It cooked quickly and he scooped it up and put a serving on their plates, but he held back a few pieces. Then he slid one small piece of shrimp onto his spatula and motioned to Martin. Martin took the cue and held his mouth open. He tensed up slightly and waited for the chef's move. While Martin held his head back slightly, the chef gave a little flick to his spatula and let the shrimp fly in a high arc. Martin made a short bob to his right and caught the shrimp neatly in his mouth, evoking a cheer from the other couples and a giggle from Maria. Then it was her turn.

"Oh, oh!" she said, grabbing Martin's arm while focusing on the chef, nodding to him that she was ready. She didn't have to move as the shrimp flew straight at her and she took it cleanly in her mouth. "All right!" She raised her glass and motioned to Martin to do the same and once again they clinked them together and drank in celebration of their shrimp catching success.

The rest of the meal was great fun for Maria as she watched the chef. The food was delicious, the drinks were tasty and the chef's show was just as entertaining to Maria as Martin had promised.

"That guy was amazing at cutting and slicing the meat. He was so fast, yet in full control," she said as they walked arm-in-arm to the Jeep.

Martin smiled down at his lovely dinner date. "He could be a knife thrower in the circus."

"Or something else."

"Like what?"

"Oh, well, maybe a latter day Jack the Ripper." Maria laughed, thinking that Ben Secani might be able to use a guy like that chef.

"That's a rather gruesome thought," replied Martin, "but I guess you're right. If I need a man who's good with a knife, I know where to look."

Maria decided it was time to change the subject. "This was great, but I hope you like other types of ethnic food, too, like Italian," she said to Martin.

"I love Italian food. I go to Govoni's in Hillsboro fairly often. Would you like to go there sometime?"

"Absolutely. I've eaten there a few times. They've got great veal!"

They stepped into the Jeep and drove back to Henniker. As they entered the highway Maria commented on how much colder it was than when they went into the restaurant. Martin turned on the heater and adjusted the temperature to a moderate level.

"How's that?"

"Much better."

"I know it's a week night, but would you care for a nightcap?"

"I'd love one."

Martin smiled at his date. "Where would you like to go?"

"Somewhere with a fireplace would be nice."

"Hmm, let me think," said Martin.

"I'll bet you've got a fireplace at your house," suggested Maria.

Martin's hands tightened around the steering wheel.

"As a matter of fact, I do." He turned to glance at Maria for a moment. She was looking right at him with a grin. He felt a slight tingle run down his spine.

Once back in Henniker, Martin steered his Jeep into the driveway and parked in front of the garage. He helped Maria out of the vehicle and took her along a stone walkway and into the dimly lit enclosed front porch. Maria gazed around at the forested property and noticed the lack of visible neighbors.

Martin opened the door and led Maria through so that he could flip on the living room light. "There's the fireplace you wanted, Maria. Let me get that nightcap for you and then I'll start a fire. How about some red wine?"

"That would be great." Maria moved to the sofa. She sat at the end nearest the fireplace and brushed her hands against her upper arms for warmth. In a moment, Martin appeared with two glasses of wine. He handed one to Maria and then went about building the fire.

"Here's my wood supply," he said as he reached into a closed box beside the hearth.

Maria let out a laugh when she saw Martin pull an artificial log out of the box, place it in the fireplace and light it at both ends.

"Modern chemistry," he laughed, "a woodsman's best friend."

Martin turned back from the fireplace and stood at the hearth looking at Maria, but saying nothing. She was watching the flame build and didn't notice his staring. He decided music would be a cure for his speechlessness and he went to his stereo on shelving under the living room window. He selected an album from his collection and showed it to Maria.

"*Rubber Soul,* okay?" he asked as he pulled the Beatle recording from its sleeve. She nodded and he began playing it, then moved to sit next to her.

The atmosphere in the room was warm and comfortable, but real estate was the best topic he could come up with for conversation.

"I'm just renting this place for now, but I think I'm going to buy it," he said, looking out the window. "The owner is getting along in years and his family doesn't use it anymore. It used to be a vacation house for them. His kids live in other states, so he's talking about selling if I want it. There's nearly sixteen acres, so I might be able to clear and develop some of it. With the new highway coming in just south of here, the property value will be going up, and I should be able to make some good money if I subdivide the lot and build a couple of houses."

"That sounds like a great idea. So, you're planning on staying here for a while, I gather."

"Yeah, I like it here. Henniker is a good town in a nice location. Living in a small college town appeals to me. It's rural, but not too isolated. It's just an hour and twenty minutes or so from Boston, so I can maintain my high level of sophistication as needed." He smiled.

"Oh, I know about that."

"That's right, I almost forgot that you're a proper Bostonian, too. Where in the city do you live, Maria?"

"I don't want to bore you with that." She quickly changed the subject. "Tell me more about your plans for this property. It sounds like you've got an interesting idea. How many houses do you plan to build on this lot?"

"Well, like I said, I'm just renting now, but if I buy it, I'll have it surveyed and see about getting it subdivided. I'd keep enough land for myself—you know, for some privacy, and maybe cut up the rest into one or two acre parcels. I'll get one of the Engineering faculty to help me out. I'm sure there's some potential there for a little free consultation. Maria, I'm really glad we had this night together. This is the best time I've had in quite a while."

The sound of *Michelle* came from the stereo and Maria responded as if on cue. "Maybe a dance would add to the enjoyment," she suggested.

Martin smiled warmly, took Maria's glass and put it along with his on the mantle over the fireplace. When he came back to her, Maria stood up and Martin took her gently in his arms. They began dancing very slowly, sliding over the hardwood floor, with Maria resting her head on Martin's shoulder, their cheeks touching lightly. His hand pressed the small of her back and she moved in more closely, pressing her warm body against him. Maria closed her eyes, but Martin's eyes remained open wide, like he'd miss out on something if he closed them. He didn't want to risk missing anything. He was in heaven.

As the music continued, Maria slid her left hand over Martin's shoulder and caressed the back of his neck. Taking the cue, Martin released Maria's right hand and wrapped both of his arms around her at the small of her back. She responded by holding both of her arms around his neck and drawing him closer. Martin felt his heart beating faster as Maria's body warmed him. He brought both of his hands to her waist and then moved them upward, caressing her sides gently. Martin thought he heard a soft moan from Maria, and he felt her squirm even closer to him. He drew his head back to look at her and she did the same, offering her lips to him. Martin kissed her gently at first, but then harder. As he was about to open his mouth, the music stopped and he backed his head away. "I'll change the record, if you like."

Maria shook her head slowly from side to side and then grabbed his hand. "There's a special room you haven't shown me," she whispered.

Taking her hint, Martin began walking toward the bedroom, his hand wrapped tightly around Maria's. They helped each other undress and climbed into his bed. Martin's joy was complete. He was making love to Maria at last.

The sound of his alarm clock startled Martin, and he hurried to turn it off. Five-thirty came without warning. He had slept soundly through the night, as had Maria.

"Oh, that's painful," she said, realizing how early it was.

"Sorry."

He sat up on the edge of the bed and started to get up when he felt Maria's arm wrap around his waist and her hand pressed firmly between his legs.

"Where do you think you're going?"

"Maria, it's Friday, I've got class, and so do you. I . . ."

He couldn't finish his sentence. Maria's hands caressed him front and back and his arousal was full.

"I guess I have enough time . . . before . . ."

Maria pulled him back onto the bed and he again found himself making love to this woman who excited him like no other.

After climaxing, the two lay beside each other and dozed off for additional sleep. When he awoke, Martin eased himself off the bed and headed for the bathroom. He started to run the shower, waiting for hot water. He gave a short jump when he felt Maria's hand on him again.

"I can't let you get in there all by yourself so early in the morning. You might drown!"

They took their time, drawing out their enjoyment as much as possible, and then they toweled off each other, relishing the contact. When they were sufficiently dry, Maria dropped her towel and walked out of the bathroom, giving Martin a chance to gaze at her fully nude. She returned to the bedroom and put her clothes back on while Martin shaved.

When Martin had dressed, he heard Maria humming something to herself in the kitchen. The smell of fresh coffee and toast filled the room. Maria was standing over the stove cooking scrambled eggs. She had made herself right at home in his kitchen, locating all items needed for their first breakfast together. Martin stood in the doorway smiling at Maria's self-sufficiency.

"You're highly competent in at least three rooms of a house," said Martin. "I can't wait to see your other talents."

"I have some you can't imagine."

"So many talents, so little time," said Martin.

They enjoyed their breakfast and then Martin realized he'd have to take Maria back to her apartment before he could go to his office for his class preparation. Maria persuaded him it wasn't necessary and that she'd meet up with him at his office after her morning classes. He could give her a ride home later. Only fair, since she gave him a lift.

Chapter Twenty-One

Martin began his nine o'clock class with an open question. "Who can tell us something about the state of the world economy in the mid 1930s?" He avoided looking straight at Maria while waiting for a response, which soon came from another student. "There was worldwide depression. It wasn't just in the United States," said the young man in the second row.

"What role did John Maynard Keynes play in that time period?" asked Martin. This time he quickly scanned the room, noticing Maria looking down. The joy and excitement she had been showing over the night suddenly disappeared into quietness, as if she had withdrawn into another world. Perhaps she was masking her true feelings for him from the other students. That would make sense. He took some relief in that logic.

Sue stood in the aisle between the rows of seats, waiting for Maria to gather up her books. As they walked out together, Maria gazed at Martin and broke into a warm smile. Martin acknowledged the look and felt a warm rush go through him. *Love is always a roller coaster ride,* he thought.

In her Economics class, Maria looked at her watch several times, realizing this was a Friday and soon she would have to leave for Boston. For the first time she didn't want to go. She was no longer just a college student. She was a woman whose life was beginning to unfold before her in a way she'd not expected. Though she'd technically lost her virginity years ago on that horrible night in East Boston, what she experienced last night was truly her first time; the first time she and a man had made love. It was like nothing she had ever known or thought she would.

Sue caught up with Maria in the cafeteria and they sat together for lunch. They went through the food line and Sue made a couple of attempts at casual conversation, but got only short replies from her friend.

"Are you okay, Maria?" They placed their food trays on their table. "You were very quiet in class this morning and you don't seem to be very talkative right now, either. Is it that time of month, or something?"

Maria forced a smile and shook her head. "I'm okay, really. I just don't feel like talking very much."

"Now don't go into denial on me. This is me, Sue, your friend, remember?"

Maria looked away from Sue for a second and then turned straight toward her from across the table. "It's not a big deal, Sue, really. Please don't make a big thing out of this, okay?" Sue nodded yes and leaned forward hoping to hear more. "I went out to dinner with Martin last night and had a wonderful time."

Sue's eyes opened wide and she gave a muffled squeal. "That's great! Did you . . ."

Maria cut her off with a raised eyebrow. "Sue, please!"

"Okay, okay. I'm sorry."

Maria resumed her explanation. "Like I said, I had a great time. Now it's Friday and I guess I'm a little down about having to go to Boston for the weekend, for the first time in I don't know when."

"Well, can't you skip it for a change, call in sick or something?"

Maria was amused at the thought of calling in sick to Ben Secani. She just shook her head no to Sue. "I'll just live with it, go to work and be back on Monday, as usual."

Her words didn't fool Sue, who could hear some real hurt in Maria's tone and in her look, but Sue knew she had reached a line she shouldn't try to cross.

After lunch, Sue drove Maria to The Inn and waited while Maria went into Martin's office. He was seated at his desk flipping through some papers when she came into the room and he looked up with a start. He stood as Maria walked around the desk and stood in front of him. As he began to speak, Maria held up her hand to stop him.

"I know what you're going to say. You're going to ask if I'm okay. Well, yes, I'm okay. I just went through an interrogation with Sue."

She reached both arms around Martin's neck and kissed him slowly, then released her grip and moved back a half step. "I want you to know that last night was fantastic. Nobody's ever made me feel the way you did, the way you do. But it's Friday and I have to go to Boston for the weekend."

Martin searched for the right words to say and finally spoke, not knowing if he had found them or not. "I know you have that Boston job, but you must be able to get some time off. I'm hoping you can go with me to Cape Cod sometime when I go to the Wampanoag Museum. I plan to interview a tribal elder for my book. It wouldn't take the whole day and then we could go to the National Seashore. We could take a great escape together."

Maria smiled briefly. "That sounds great, Martin, and I hope we can do it. I just don't know when. I need to try to work some things out. I need you to be patient with me. Can you?"

"Of course. I won't get in the way of whatever else you have to do, with whomever."

Maria looked stunned by Martin's last words. He was an adult, after all. It wasn't hard for him to figure out that her business in Boston must include someone significant in her life.

Maria walked slowly toward the office door and then looked back at Martin. He was still standing behind his desk following her every move, admiring a beauty he now saw as being much deeper than just physical.

"Sue's going to give me a lift to my apartment. I'll be back Monday."

"I'll be right here."

Reassured, Maria threw a kiss at him before she left the room.

Maria arrived in Boston at about four o'clock and was able to find a curbside parking place only a block away from her building. Henniker had spoiled her. She didn't notice the two men in a car across the street watching her arrive.

Although it was a pleasant fall day, the air was stuffy in Maria's apartment, so she opened windows in the living room and bedroom. An inspection of the refrigerator told her she'd have to make a quick trip to the local market. She made a mental note of the things she'd need. After a snack, a glass of cola and a brief rest, Maria grabbed her purse and a fold-up shopping cart and headed off to the market. Although she was tired, she wanted to stretch her legs after the drive from New Hampshire. She could relax after restocking her kitchen.

*****

With Leo beside him, Jack Contino pulled his police car alongside the unmarked surveillance vehicle on Marlborough Street across from Maria Falcone's apartment. He got out and entered the other car's backseat. Leo Barbado slid into the driver's seat of the car and drove off slowly.

"You got here quick," said the man behind the steering wheel.

"Yeah, I've got a big date," said Jack.

"I think your girl has arrived. We saw someone who fits the description. I was beginning to think she didn't exist. She just left on foot with a shopping cart, like she's been away for a while and she needs some groceries. I imagine she'll be back in a jiffy."

Leo appeared on foot a few minutes later, having parked on another block. He got into the backseat with Jack.

"Seems our girl has gone on a quick trip to the market. We'll wait here until she gets back. Roll down your window, would you, Leo? With four badass cops in here, we need a little air."

The four cops settled back in their seats, hoping Maria Falcone's shopping trip wouldn't take long.

Their patience was rewarded in less than ten minutes. They spied an attractive young woman in tight jeans and a red sweatshirt pulling a wheeled shopping cart with two brown bags in it. "That's her," said Jack's stakeout man.

"Let's let her get inside. Then, we'll get acquainted," said Jack. Leo acknowledged his partner. The big detective forced his large frame out of the backseat. By the time he was on his feet, Leo was already standing beside him, smirking. Jack just scowled and said, "Come on."

The men walked quickly across the street, entered into the mailbox lobby and rang the bell for the apartment reading *M. Falcone* over the mailbox. Jack rubbed his hands together in anticipation. Leo rocked back and forth on his feet.

Maria was startled by the sound of the doorbell as she put the bags of groceries on her kitchen counter. *Who could that be?* Ben wouldn't ring the bell, since he had his own key. Certainly no client would stop by unexpected. Reluctantly, Maria went to her front door and pushed the reply button. "Who's there?"

"Detectives Contino and Barbado, MDC Police. We're looking for Maria Falcone."

Maria felt a chill and she paused for a moment before answering.

"I'm Maria. What's this about?"

"We'd just like to talk to you, Miss Falcone. May we come up?"

Maria said nothing as she pushed the button that opened the lobby door.

Jack and Leo jogged up the first few steps and then slowed to a walk, climbing to the third floor. They found the apartment and knocked. The door opened partway as Maria kept the chain lock in place. Jack looked down at the beautiful young woman with dark hair and blue eyes, more nervous and vulnerable looking than he'd expect from a high priced call girl connected to the Mob.

"Hello, Miss Falcone. I'm Detective Contino. As I said, we'd just like to ask you a few questions. Could we please come in?"

Maria hesitated. This police contact was not like when she learned of her father's death. A strong sense of reality set in. After all these years she finally began to appreciate that there were risks involved and a price to be paid.

"I guess it would be okay," said Maria slowly.

She fumbled with the lock, but she eventually got it open and swung the door wide to let the two detectives in. They looked all around as they moved into the living room. It just seemed like a young woman's apartment, not a house for illegal activities. Jack noticed a number of hardcover books on her shelf and one stood out for him. He slid it halfway out of its place on the shelf, handling it lightly with his big hands.

"You must have been about what, twelve or thirteen when JFK was killed?" he said, staring at William Manchester's *Death of a President* as if he'd just been taken on a quick trip back in time. John Kennedy had been a hero of his.

"About that age. What did you want to talk to me about?" she asked, steering the detective back to the business at hand, anxious for this visit to end.

"How well do you know Ben Secani, Miss Falcone?" asked Leo abruptly.

Jack sent a glance over to Leo. Before she could answer, Jack said, "We know he rents this apartment, Miss Falcone, so we gather you know him fairly well. Please, what can you tell us about him?"

Jack knew his size could intimidate a small young woman like Maria, especially with another cop by his side.

"Is it okay if we sit down?" Sitting would neutralize the size difference and help ease the tension.

Maria nodded and sat in a chair. Jack and Leo took seats on the sofa facing her.

Maria thought carefully before answering the detective's question about Ben.

"I know him. I've known him for years. He's an old family friend from East Boston. His mom took me in when my dad passed away. I was still in high school. She's a wonderful lady, his mom."

Jack looked down for a second. "What about your mom, Maria? Where was she when your father died?"

Maria was surprised that he'd called her by her first name and she felt more at ease when he did. "Oh, she had left well before that."

Jack noticed a pained expression on her face, but it passed quickly.

"What does my mom have to do with this?"

"I'm sorry. I was just trying to clarify why you moved in with Ben Secani's mother."

The room was silent for a moment. Maria perched on the front edge of her chair and rubbed her hands against her arms.

"Maria, when was the last time you saw Ben Secani?" asked Jack softly. He was endeavoring to keep the young woman from shutting up altogether.

"It was a couple of weeks ago. You never did tell me what this is all about. Why do you want to know so much about Ben? Is he in some trouble?"

"We're not sure, but we have reason to believe he may have been involved in an incident a few weeks ago. His name came up. It may mean nothing. We're just trying to put the puzzle together."

"What incident, where?"

Jack felt himself losing control of this interrogation. The young woman was reversing the roles all of a sudden. *Time to cut your losses,* he thought. He reached inside his jacket pocket and pulled out a business card. He reached toward Maria and handed it to her, and then he and Leo stood up in unison.

"You've been very cooperative, Maria, and we appreciate it. If you ever want to contact me, my office and home phone numbers are on the card. Feel free to call me any time of day."

Yeah, that's what they always say in the TV detective shows, thought Maria. Maybe she'd call him at home at three in the morning sometime, just to test him. Bet his wife would love that!

"We can let ourselves out," said Leo.

As they reached the sidewalk, Jack looked at Leo. "Are you any relation to Don Rickles—you know, Mr. Warmth? You've got about as much tact!"

"Hey, I asked a legit question."

"I know. I know. But sometimes it's not what you say, but how you say it. This kid's no hard case. I think she's a victim of circumstances and maybe she's made some bad choices in her life. If we take it easy with her, we'll probably get a lot further than if we play tough cop."

"I hope so, because we didn't get very far this time."

"That's all right. This won't be the last time we talk to her."

The men made their way over to the surveillance car and told the other detectives to go home. They had their ID on Maria and her apartment. Besides, she probably had checked them out through the window as they left the building.

˙˙˙˙

The detectives left quietly and Maria sat in the chair looking at the business card. She got up slowly and went into the kitchen. She put the card in her purse and then poured herself a glass of wine from an open bottle on her kitchen counter. Her eyes began to fill with tears and she felt a chill like none she had ever felt before.

What should she do? She couldn't call Ben. They might have her phone tapped. This would surely set Ben off, and nothing really happened. She didn't tell them anything important. *Surely they know a lot more about him than they were letting on,* she thought. *But what if he comes by tonight for his usual? Maybe I could put him off for the night. Remember what Sue said about calling in sick? That was it. Call him and say you're not well. Give yourself time to get collected. Tomorrow you'll be ready for business.*

Maria composed herself and grabbed her purse to make sure she had some change in it, then she left the apartment once again. She didn't bother to look at the cop car as she headed down the street to the market. The phone booth outside was not being used, so she rushed the last few yards to claim it. She dropped a quarter into the pay phone and dialed Ben's number. There was no answer, so she tried Club 77 and found him.

"Hi, Ben. It's me, Maria," she said, sounding weak, as intended.

"Hi, Baby, what's up? You seem kinda low."

"Yeah, I had a rough trip down from New Hampshire. I've got some sort of flu bug and had to make a couple of stops along the way."

"Maybe I can come by and cheer you up, Baby,"

"No, no. You shouldn't come over tonight. I can't stray too far from the toilet, you know what I mean? You don't want to catch this one."

Ben's tone stopped being playful. "Oh, I see what you mean. Yeah, I can do without that trouble. I sure hope you'll be okay for tomorrow night. You know Mr. Sullivan s in town and he's hoping to see you. Call me here around noon tomorrow and let me know how you're feeling, okay?"

"Yeah. Sure. I'll call." She was about to hang up when a car drove by and honked its horn as a cab cut into its lane. Maria realized Ben could certainly hear that. "I'm at the market getting some Pepto," she said quickly covering herself. "I got to get back quick."

"Okay. Talk to you soon. Get better, Babe."

Maria went into the market and bought the medicine so it would be visible in the apartment if Ben did show up. Relieved that she'd succeeded in putting Ben off, she went back to her apartment to consider her next move. She had at least bought herself some time to think.

ƒ ƒ ƒ ƒ

Leo Barbado drove the cop car back to the office in South Boston while Jack sat in the front passenger seat tapping his fingers on his knee. Leo knew Jack was thinking about his next move. "You making strategy, partner?" he asked.

"We're going to have to squeeze this one gently."

Leo snickered at the possible double meaning to that statement.

Jack looked at him harshly. "Clean it up, Leo. You know what I mean."

Leo backed off. Unlike many of his colleagues, Jack had never strayed. He was a devoted family man, and Leo respected that. But he couldn't pass up a chance to have a little fun. Jack made such a great straight man.

Chapter Twenty-Two

Maria slept until just after seven o'clock in the morning, then she climbed out of bed wearing only an old Red Sox T-shirt that Ben had given her. It suited her just fine as sleepwear. The overnight rest had made her feel much better, and she wandered into the kitchen to make her breakfast.

The smell of scrambled eggs and sausage cooking on the stove along with wheat bread in her toaster took her mind off the problem she would have to address later in the day. She brewed some coffee, adding to the kitchen aroma. When all the food was ready, she placed a filled dish on the table and went into the living room to flip on her stereo. After tuning in a good FM station, Maria went back to the kitchen to enjoy her breakfast in peace.

In a few moments her thoughts returned to her visit from the police. She sipped her coffee and thought about what the big cop had said. Ben was involved in an incident recently. *No, no. His name came up. That was what he had said. An incident took place and Ben's name came up. How does a name come up? Did they talk to somebody else about the incident? Was it the four man murder that happened the night Ben left her near midnight and came back the next morning?* Now she was convinced he'd been involved. A chill ran down her spine for a moment and she sipped more coffee to warm herself. She believed Ben was capable of killing. Of course, he was. He'd killed in the war, and the rumors about him during her high school years were that he was a Mob hit man. She had always laughed at those rumors, but not anymore. Four men!

Maria ate some food, had more coffee and paced the floor, as if she was working a jigsaw puzzle in her head. Ben killed four guys that night and he needed an alibi. She was it. It was the only time Ben asked her to make an alibi for him. *If anybody asks,* he'd said, *tell them he spent the night here with me.* That would involve her in the murder. She would be an accessory. That would be far worse than being a call girl if she were caught in such a lie. She could go to prison. *Think this out carefully,* she thought to herself, beginning to tremble. *Try to stay cool.*

It was a crisp fall morning and Maria felt the cold as she pulled off her T-shirt and walked naked from her bedroom to the shower. After dressing in tan Levi jeans and a baggy blue sweater, Maria grabbed her purse and left her building for a walk. Perhaps the smell of the city on a fall morning would help her think. After taking a few steps along the sidewalk Maria stopped suddenly. Looking straight ahead, she wondered if the MDC cops were back on her street. *Don't look around,* she told herself. *If they are back, screw them.*

Why would Ben kill those men, she thought. He didn't have to have a reason if he was a hit man. He was probably just doing a job, but who would give him such an assignment? Maybe that guy who owned the Club77, Joe Vito? Ben said he worked for that guy. Was Vito the boss? Maybe somebody else, but maybe it was him. *What could those four guys have done to deserve being murdered? They did something the boss didn't like. I guess you don't cross Mr. Vito.*

❧ ❧ ❧ ❧

Ginny had been sound asleep until she felt the weight of Ben's body on top of her once again. She groaned softly and Ben took it as a sign that he was once again pleasing her with his manliness. He didn't see her clenched fist, nor her grimace as he continued thrusting inside her. The experience was brief, sort of like a morning constitutional for Ben, devoid of any passion or concern for his partner. Ginny just suited his purpose when Maria wasn't available. Good old Ginny.

As Ben rolled off of her and onto his back, Ginny sat up on the edge of the bed and reached for the cigarettes on the night table. She lit one up and sat there for a moment taking some long drags. Ben smelled the smoke and looked over at Ginny. He smiled while thinking about the old cliché about smoking after sex. *That was her dessert,* he thought to himself.

"You're really terrific, sweetie," he said to her, waiting for the return compliment.

"You're great, too, Ben." She stood up and started to walk out of the room. "I gotta go pee."

Ben grabbed the phone next to the bed and dialed Maria's number. She picked up after four rings.

"Hi, kid. How are you feeling today? I hope I didn't disturb you on the throne."

Maria paused before replying. "I'm okay, Ben. I feel much better. No, you didn't disturb anything. I was just doing some studying, that's all."

"Good, I'm glad to hear it. So you'll be okay for your date tonight with Wayne Sullivan. He's looking forward to a real good time with you and maybe he'll be even more generous than before."

Maria was glad he couldn't see her face. "Yeah, I'll be ready for him."

"You sure you're okay? You want me to stop over? You sound a little sluggish."

"Hey, you'd be sluggish, too, if you spent last night like I did. If you don't mind, I'd really just like to finish my schoolwork and get some more rest. I want to be at my best for Mr. Sullivan, especially if he's going to be in a giving mood."

Ben chuckled at her comment and then nodded as if she could see him over the phone. "I guess you're right again, kid. You take care of yourself, and be sure to give Mr. Sullivan a real good time tonight. I'll see you tomorrow to check on his generosity." Ben expected a reply from Maria, but only got the click sound of her phone being hung up.

Ginny called out from the hallway as she left the bathroom and walked back toward the bedroom. "Who you talkin' to, Ben, that little honey of yours in the Back Bay?"

Ben sprang out of bed, took two steps toward Ginny and in a fluid motion grabbed her under her arms and lifted her up in front of him while walking to the bathroom. Her leg brushed his penis and he stiffened again.

"Hey, what are you doin'?"

"Shower time," he laughed. "I believe in the buddy system."

# Connections	Steven P. Marini

❦ ❦ ❦ ❦

The evening arrived too soon for Maria, but she had to deal with the inevitable. She put on a dress very similar to the one she had worn on her last date with Mr. Sullivan, only this time it was basic black. She greeted his call at her door and accepted his high praise for her beautiful appearance. Then they were in his limousine with Wayne pouring drinks from the bar cabinet.

"Scotch, neat," he said, recalling Maria's choice of beverage from before. "I think you'll find this single malt quite acceptable."

Maria forced a smile and took the glass in her hand. Sullivan sat back beside her with his drink and held it out toward hers. They clinked glasses ceremoniously and sipped the fine Scotch whiskey.

Wayne reached for a control panel near his seat, pushed a couple of buttons and sat back with Maria close by his side. His hand found the slit in her dress, and his fingers caressed her thigh as the voice of a young Frank Sinatra filled the limo with soft tones.

"I thought you'd like this early Sinatra music." He was eager to know he was pleasing his young companion.

"Yes, I love that sound." She let her head fall back on the seat cushion. She closed her eyes momentarily, getting lost in the sweet tone of the music. She escaped mentally to a quiet, simple and peaceful place, oblivious to the man's hand moving up the inner part of her thigh as far as he could go and back down again. Maria paid no attention at first to the direction of the limo as it headed north on Storrow Drive. Within minutes it had merged onto I-93 southbound.

"You know, Maria, you made my last trip to Boston very worthwhile. You're a most remarkable young woman. Everything about you pleases me. If I were a young man I might try to take you away with me. But I'm a realist, and know that I'll just have to settle for these wonderful visits with you."

Maria spoke with her head still back and her eyes closed. "You're very kind, Mr. Sullivan."

Suddenly she felt his hand squeeze her leg gently and she opened her eyes.

"It's Wayne, remember?"

"Er, yes, Wayne. I'm sorry."

Suddenly her interest shifted to the direction the limo was taking. She looked out the darkened window which gave a clear view from inside. "What's our destination tonight, Wayne?" She tried to hide any sign of nervousness.

"There's a wonderful restaurant in North Providence with the best Italian food. Sinatra has eaten there himself. You're going to love it."

Maria again leaned back in her seat. It seemed she couldn't escape Italian food wherever she was. Wayne put his drink down and slid his arm around Maria, coaxing her closer to him.

"If you're tired, dear, just relax and close your eyes if you wish. We have about thirty minutes to get there, so take a rest here close to me."

Maria complied with his suggestion, since she didn't really feel like making conversation with her customer. She withdrew into a private world while Wayne's hand found her breasts. It was a fair trade-off.

Maria benefited from the rest period, but soon they were at the curb of The Roman Grille in North Providence. The driver opened their door and Maria slid out of the limo before Wayne. A big smile appeared on Wayne's face as they passed through the lobby and came face-to-face with a large picture on the wall showing Frank Sinatra shaking hands with an older man in chef's garb. Sinatra had autographed the photo. *Vic, your pasta is unbeatable, Frank.*

"He visits Providence now and then, and he always comes to The Roman for a dinner," said Wayne.

"I'm impressed."

"Good evening, Mr. Sullivan," said a tall, husky man in a black tuxedo. "It's so good to see you again."

"It's great to be here, Victor," answered Wayne.

The two men clasped hands in a warm greeting, and Wayne introduced Victor to Maria. Victor was used to seeing beautiful young women accompanying his older, well-heeled customers. They were immediately seated at a corner table for two.

❦ ❦ ❦ ❦

Leo Barbado pulled his car up to within a half block of Jack Contino's brown sedan and parked along the curb. He got out, walked up to Jack's car, and got in the back.

"Good job, partner," said Jack, looking across the street at the limo in front of The Roman Grille. "He has no idea he's been followed all the way from Boston. The two-car method works every time, especially at night. Hey, are you hungry? I've got a couple of sandwiches here and some coffee."

"Your wife is a saint!" declared Leo, eyeballing the homemade food and a thermos.

"This is going to take a while. We might as well get comfortable and chow down. I wonder what they're having!" Jack laughed. "I don't think it's tuna on wheat."

❦ ❦ ❦ ❦

Maria's mood seemed to improve as they enjoyed their dinner. Victor stopped by their table and regaled Wayne with stories of visits by Frank Sinatra and the members of his family, who sometimes accompanied him to The Roman Grille. "It must be a thrill for you to have him dine here," she said.

The stories, the dinner and the tiramisu took Maria's mind off of things temporarily. Soon, however, she would be back in the limo with Wayne, headed for the toughest part of the night.

Maria excused herself and made a trip to the ladies room. It could be a long trip back to Boston. As she crossed the floor on her return, she was distracted by the sound of a familiar male voice. She looked around while walking but didn't see anyone she knew. Still, the voice was familiar. She lowered her head and put her hand up to her face to offer some cover. She had no desire to be recognized.

After taking her seat, she grabbed Wayne's hand across the table. "Perhaps we should be getting back," she said, a hint of playfulness in her voice. She wasn't really feeling playful, but she wanted to avoid whoever it was in the restaurant who might know her, and she wanted to finish her business with Wayne.

"I couldn't agree more." Wayne was quite pleased by Maria's suggestion. "Let me visit the little boy's room and we'll be off."

Maria sat nervously toying with her napkin while Wayne paid his respects to Victor on his way back to the table. The maître d' walked with him so that he could see Maria up close one more time. He took her hand as she stood, and he kissed it warmly, wishing her good night. Another old guy putting his mouth on her skin! After her wonderful night with Martin, such an experience, to which she'd always been indifferent, was now distasteful.

Wayne hurried them into his limo and instructed his driver to make it a slow ride back to Boston. The limo retraced its earlier route and headed north on I-95. Wayne's pace, though, became quicker. His hands fondled Maria. He kissed her lips, her cheek, her neck. Evidently, she was to perform her services in the limo.

*****

Jack Contino followed at a distance, watching their target slide into the right hand lane and travel at fifty miles per hour. He slowed his car down, too, but stayed in the middle lane, confused by the driver's strange behavior. Leo's voice came over the radio.

"Hey, what's going on? Do you think he made you, Jack? Over."

"No, but I'd better be careful, Leo. I'll pass him and move up to the rest area a couple of miles ahead. I'll pull back in after you pass and I'll drop behind you. Over."

"Okay," said Leo. "But it sure seems like he's up to something. Out."

Jack accelerated past the limo, and Leo pressed his gas pedal until he was at a good trailing distance. The rest of the trip to Boston was uneventful.

Once back in the city, Jack instructed Leo to go ahead to Maria's apartment and park nearby. They stayed in radio contact, in case there was a change in destination. Leo was to let the limo pull up and not make a move until Maria emerged.

The limo stopped, double parking in front of Maria's building, and came to a quiet stop.

"Once again, you have pleased me beyond words, Maria," said Wayne as he tucked in his shirt, leaving his necktie and jacket on the floor. He slipped on his shoes and helped Maria zip up her dress in the back. Then Wayne picked up his jacket and took out a thick envelope, stuffed with cash and gave it to Maria.

"You're very generous, Mr. Sull . . . excuse me, Wayne. Thank you very much."

"Believe me, my wife costs a lot more than what's in that envelope! You're worth every penny!"

The driver then stepped out onto the street and opened the passenger door, not noticing at first the police car with its lights off pulling up behind them. Leo reacted quickly and ran to the limo as Maria exited the plush vehicle with Wayne Sullivan right behind her, sliding his hand over her backside.

"Hope you all had a pleasant evening," said Jack, flashing his badge at the driver. "I think you need to get back in the driver's seat and remain very cool, young man." He motioned toward the front of the limo.

Seeing the second police officer arriving, the driver wasn't about to argue.

Leo snatched Maria's purse from her hands and opened it, finding the envelope with a handsome amount of cash in it.

"Hey, what the hell are you doing?" snapped Maria.

"Maria, you just stand there with Detective Barbado and be quiet for a moment. I need to have a word with Mr. . . . sorry, I didn't catch the name."

"Sullivan," said Wayne. "Wayne Sullivan." His left knee twitched.

"I'd like to see some identification, Mr. Sullivan."

Wayne motioned to the limo. "My wallet is in my jacket in the car."

"Get it." Jack pushed back his coat to reveal his weapon. "Just make sure that's all you get."

"There's no need for that," said Wayne, his voice beginning to crack.

"I hope not. I'll be watching you, just the same."

Wayne did as directed.

Wayne shivered as Jack put his big hand on Wayne's shoulder, turned him away from the others and moved a few steps up the sidewalk. "Walk with me, Mr. Sullivan."

They strode about twenty feet away from the limo. Jack took out a pen and notepad and wrote down Wayne's name and address from his driver's license as they walked.

"Just so we can keep in touch," said Jack, noticing that Wayne seemed surprised by Jack's action. Once he had finished writing, Jack put the notepad and pen away, folded his arms across his chest and stood face-to-face with Wayne.

"Here's the way it is, Mr. Sullivan. We're not in the least bit interested in you. I hope you got your money's worth because it's the last time you're going to see this young woman . . . the very last time. The next time you come to this city, you're going to have to get your entertainment somewhere else. If you try to see this kid again, it could get you into more trouble than you can imagine, so don't ever make me get interested in you, understand?"

Wayne nodded.

"Tell whoever you used to arrange your date with her that it just didn't work out. Tell him your wife is getting suspicious or something. I wouldn't tell him what actually happened tonight. That could get you into trouble with the bad guys, so you'd be at risk from both ends, get it? Now, you're going to get in your car and leave quietly. Goodnight, Mr. Sullivan, and I hope this is goodbye."

Wayne scurried back to his limo and jumped into the passenger section without so much as a glance at Maria. He told his driver to get moving and reached for a glass, pouring himself a Scotch as the limo cruised away into the night. Maria's business with Wayne Sullivan was over.

Walking back to Maria and Leo, Jack motioned to his partner to go to his car. Jack opened the back door, took Maria by the arm and helped her into the seat, sliding in beside her while Leo took his place behind the wheel.

"Am I under arrest?" she asked without looking at anybody. She swallowed hard.

Jack's voice became soft. "Maria, you need to listen to me very carefully. Do you understand?"

Slowly, she raised her head up and looked at Jack, a worried expression on her face.

"Maria, you're involved with some very dangerous people. Your connection to Ben Secani goes much deeper than you know. You do business with him and he does business with other people, bad people. You're going to give him a large chunk of the money that's in that envelope. That makes him happy. But he's got to give some of it to somebody else up the chain to keep that guy happy. That's how it works."

Maria looked away without speaking. She knew Jack was talking about Mr. Vito, or somebody like him, who associated with Ben. What a different world it was in Boston from the one she knew in New Hampshire! If only she could have one and not the other!

"That's why we're not going to confiscate that money tonight, and we're not going to arrest you."

Maria looked at Jack and then turned her head away, raising her hand to her mouth, biting softly on her knuckle. "Oh, my God. So, you're setting a trap, and I'm the bait!"

There was a stark silence for a moment as Jack and Leo saw their plan for Maria from her point of view for a change. Maria broke the silence.

"You know what I do during the week, Detective? I go to college in New Hampshire. I'm just a student up there, a very good student. I have friends there. I'm even starting to see a guy, a professor—a single professor. I want to make a life—a real life, maybe with him. I don't know! Now I'm just a piece of cheese, bait to help you guys catch your rats."

Jack squirmed in his seat, feeling Maria's vulnerability, and wished there was another way. But there wasn't. "Maria, maybe we can help you find that real life, eventually, after you've helped us. We've done it before. It's not easy, but it can be done."

"What if I don't want to play your game, Detective, then what?"

Jack looked at Leo and then back at Maria. "Then we arrest you on prostitution charges. We call back Mr. Sullivan and give him immunity to testify against you. He goes home and you get to do some time in prison. Neither your professor, nor Ben Secani, will like that very much, so the cost will be more than just some time in the klink. But it doesn't have to be that way. Look, I'm sorry this is happening to you, but you've got to take responsibility for your own decisions. You made a bad one when you snuggled up to Ben Secani."

"I grew up with Ben in my neighborhood. He was a friend of the family, and he was always good to me and my dad. He helped keep some punks away from me when I was, you know, growing."

"Okay. He was a friend, but then he made a bad career decision and you tagged along with him. Well, you're on our team now. You really don't have much choice. We need to get some information from you."

Jack jotted down Maria's address and phone number at New Sussex College, her class schedule and the make and license number of her car. He saw her expression and felt she was sufficiently scared to be truthful.

"What's next?" she asked, stifling tears.

"What time is your boyfriend coming by for the money?" asked Leo.

Maria looked at him.

"No, don't worry. We're not going to pounce on him yet. What time?"

"Hard to tell. He usually pops in anytime he wants. Could be tonight. Could be tomorrow. Could be three o'clock in the morning."

"He's going to expect his share of that dough," said Jack. "So you handle it the way you normally would." He began to spell it out for her. "Maria, we want you to get in deeper with Secani. Get to know what he's doing, who he reports to and what involvement he had in the gangland massacre that included the newspaper reporter. You remember that one in the news, don't you?"

Maria's looked down.

Jack thought he saw an opportunity. "Secani was involved in that, wasn't he?"

"I don't know that. He doesn't tell me anything. If I try to get close to his business he just pushes me away, sometimes physically. He's not going to like it if I get nosy."

"You're a clever girl, Maria. Try to find a way. We'll check back with you every now and then to hear what you've got. Remember, Maria, your future depends on how well you can help us. We need more than what you can read in the newspapers. We need someone on the inside, and that's you. Now, go upstairs and get some rest. Get yourself ready for when Secani shows up. Think about how you'll deal with him this time. Good luck."

Jack let Maria out of the car and walked her to her door. He returned to his car after she went in and he replaced Leo behind the wheel. "Go on home, Leo. I'll go back to headquarters and write this up. I'll talk to you tomorrow."

Leo returned to his car and followed his partner's advice.

Jack took a deep breath as he started his car and pulled away from Maria's building. He felt bad for Maria but, at the same time, he took great satisfaction in his police work tonight. An important door had just been opened.

Chapter Twenty-Three

Ben drove over to Maria's, let himself in and found her on the living room sofa dressed in tight-fitting blue warm up pants with a white stripe down each leg. A red T-shirt accentuated her breasts. Her bare feet made no noise on the floor as she hurried over to greet him with a hug.

"Oh, Ben. I'm so glad to see you," she said before kissing him full on the lips.

"I'm glad to see you, too, Baby," he replied, holding her in his arms and patting her ass with both hands. Ginny was good, but Maria was the real thing. "You seem to be over that flu bug, or whatever you had."

"Oh yeah, that's gone. I'm feeling much better. I even got a good night's sleep last night, since we were done so early." She lied.

"Hmmm, why early?"

"Well, Mr. Sullivan was a short ball hitter last night. He took me down to a great Italian place in Providence, but he couldn't wait to get back to Boston. He had to pop his cork in the limo. So, he just brought me back here. He was spent."

"I'm not surprised about Sullivan. I think he really has the hots for you, from what you've told me. I think he'd dump his old lady and marry you if he could. I'd better watch out for that rich bastard!" Ben forced a laugh.

"You want a cup of coffee or something?" asked Maria, walking toward the kitchen. Ben nodded and followed her. The sight of her magnificent body in the tight warm ups put Ben right into his usual mood when visiting Maria. In the kitchen, he followed her to the coffee maker and wrapped his arms around her from behind.

"Since you finished so early last night, it's been a long time since you had some real lovin'."

"Hey, I thought you wanted some coffee."

"Yeah, but I'll take my sugar first."

Ben caressed Maria, then spun her around, scooped her up in his arms and carried her to the bedroom. He took his time undressing her on the bed and then stripped himself slowly, as if he were putting on a show for his private audience. Sex with Maria was always more intense than with the other girls. She was the best.

When they were finished, they both fell into a deep sleep. About an hour later, Maria awoke and turned toward Ben. who was lying flat on his back. She snuggled up to him, draping her leg across his thighs and caressing his chest. His erection developed quickly and she climbed on top of him just as his eyes were opening. When he realized what was happening, he took hold of her breasts and smiled at her. "Boy, at first I thought I was dreaming."

Maria just smiled. "Every man's dream, Baby. Every man's dream." She glided up and down on him until Ben exploded into her.

Maria collapsed flat on her back, as if resting after an athletic event. After a long minute she spoke to him, while staring at the ceiling. "Ben, if it weren't for these times with you, doing it with customers gets to be a real drag."

"You're pretty great, yourself, Baby," said Ben, giving his usual response to a partner's compliment in bed.

"Maybe, next weekend Ben, I could take time off from our business and just spend it with you."

Ben smiled, but said nothing, still savoring his climax.

"You could use a break, too, Ben. Really. We could even get out of town overnight. Go somewhere. What do you think?"

"Get out of town? I make a lot of money here over the weekends. I'm not so sure I like the idea of getting out of Boston. There's a lot at stake. What makes you so interested in getting away? Don't you like this set-up anymore?"

"I'm not talking about anything permanent. I just think it would be great if we could have a change of pace once in awhile. That's all. Don't you ever get the urge to do something different, to go someplace different?"

Ben lay on his back, one arm around Maria, while his other hand was behind his head. "To be honest, I never really thought about it. I like it here. I make plenty of cash in the city, and I have no big urge to see the world. I saw 'Nam. That was enough."

Maria kissed Ben's chest and stroked his belly slowly. "Maybe there's more to it than the money."

"What's that supposed to mean?"

"Nothing. I just don't know what the great fascination is with the Zone and Club 77. Maybe you should educate me—you know, let me spend some time with you there."

"And when, pray tell, are you going to have the time to do that? You're away during the week and when you're in Boston you're earning your keep. Besides, you're not cut out for the Zone."

"Well, maybe I could be. I'd like to meet some of the people who make it such a fascinating place for you. That way I could get a change of scenery and you could stay in your world. What's wrong with that?"

Ben was starting to get annoyed with Maria's persistence. "What's wrong is that you have to earn your keep, like I said a minute ago."

"Ben, I earn more than that for you. You know that. A night off wouldn't hurt you."

"Hey, you forget there are other people involved in this action."

"Well, maybe I should meet them."

Ben said nothing. He didn't like where this conversation was going. What had brought all this on?

Maria was startled by Ben's sudden movement. He sat up quickly, turned around and sprang to his feet. "Let's hit the shower, kid, we've got things to do." Without looking at her, he waved her on with his index finger and she followed him quickly into the bathroom.

Ben had a plan for dealing with Maria's behavior. He got dressed quickly and took the thick envelope full of cash from Maria's dresser. He smiled as he counted out the amounts for him and Maria. Mr. Sullivan had been very generous, resulting in a few hundred dollars extra for Maria and even more for Ben and his boss. Maria slipped into a tight mini-skirt and snug-fitting white turtleneck.

"Where are we going, Ben?"

"To give you a change of scenery."

In a short time they were driving through the Combat Zone. As they passed a club with a big neon sign out front that read Di Nardi's, Ben pointed to it.

"See that club? I own ten percent."

"Ten percent. Who owns the other ninety?"

Boy, thought Ben, *she doesn't miss a beat.* "My boss, Mr. Vito. You've heard me mention his name before. Want to meet him?"

"Okay."

"He's probably at Club 77 by now." Ben steered his car along the street. When they reached Club 77, he pulled up behind a big black Cadillac parked right in front. Those two spots were never taken by any other cars without Joe Vito's permission.

Ben and Maria walked up to the front door. Ben took out his keys and found the one that unlocked the entrance. The club was dark and quiet as they moved inside. The bartender waved to them from behind the bar, where he was washing glasses.

"That's Big Ted," said Ben, his way of introducing her to the bartender.

"Hi, Big Ted," Maria said with a coy smile as she waved back to him.

Big Ted put his glass down on the bar, stood motionless and gazed at the beauty in the brief, tight clothes as she followed Ben to Joe Vito's office.

Ben knocked on the office door and motioned for Maria to stand back a few feet. He didn't know if Joe Vito was in conference or not. Joe opened the door and he looked at Ben with a smile. Then he noticed Maria and his face went blank.

"Joe," said Ben, "this is Maria Falcone, my . . . business associate."

Joe looked her up and down before offering his hand with a polite smile. "Hello, Maria. Come on in, please."

"Thank you, Mr. Vito. Ben has mentioned your name to me. It's nice to finally meet his boss."

Joe shot a quick look at Ben.

The three of them moved into the office. Joe offered drinks to Ben and Maria, which they accepted, Scotch neat for all.

"So, what brings you to Club 77, kids?"

"Maria just wanted to see where I do some of my business and meet some of my colleagues," said Ben.

"Well, she's not going to meet many people on a Sunday afternoon in here."

"Yes . . . well, Maria doesn't have much free time and she has to get back to school in New Hampshire soon," said Ben.

"Ben's told me about you," said Joe. "You go to college up north and you're Ben's business associate on the weekends, a very good arrangement."

"Yes, we all seem to benefit nicely from it." Maria's voice had a little edge to it.

They talked some more, finished their drinks and then Joe gave a strong hint that it was time to end this visit. He'd speak to Ben later about it.

"That was cool," said Maria as they got in Ben's car and headed back to her apartment.

"Joe's a good guy. He works hard, but he can play hard sometimes, too. He likes party girls."

Maria smiled at the suggestion in Ben's voice.

As they drove up to Maria's block, she spoke in a hesitant manner. "I have to go back to New Hampshire tonight, Ben. I have a test first thing in the morning, so I'd really better get back to study and be fresh tomorrow."

"Okay, I understand. You've given me quite a lot today already."

Ben stopped his T-Bird in front of her door and turned to her. She reached her arms around his neck and kissed him on the lips, slowly pressing her tongue into his mouth. Then she quickly pulled back and exited the car, waving to him as she ran up the steps of her building.

A few minutes later, Ben was back at Club 77 and in Joe Vito's office.

"Okay, Ben, what was that little visit with your *business associate* all about? I'm not sure I like it."

"Well, I'm just trying to keep my partner contented. She started talking a little strangely today. Said she wanted us to take some time off, maybe go away for a weekend. I didn't buy it so she changed her mind. Instead, she said she wanted to get to know more about my other business interests, like things in the Zone. She said that might give her enough of a change of scenery and I could stay close to my interests."

"Why does she want to know more about the Zone? She's a call girl, not a street hooker. A college girl wants to know more about this area and the people you know? It doesn't add up. Did she talk like this before?"

"No."

"So this just came out of the blue. I don't like it."

"Well, to be honest, it rattled me a little, too. That's why I brought her here today. I figured there wouldn't be much going on and a quick visit would keep her happy and no harm done."

"Yeah, well, just the same, don't bring her around here again. I don't care for her sudden curiosity."

Chapter Twenty-Four

It only took a couple of days from the time Jack Contino called Agent Nelson for the FBI to set up wiretaps at Club 77, Di Nardi's and Maria Falcone's apartment. Jack didn't like having one in Maria's place for fear he'd lose her trust if she discovered it, but it would be a mistake not to do it. He needed as many traps for Secani and Vito as he could get. Once the taps were in place, it was time for Jack and Leo to start applying some pressure.

Jack enjoyed a full dinner at home on Thursday night and complimented his wife on her usual fine cooking. "That was great, Nat, as usual. You make a killer meatloaf."

Natalie Contino smiled, accepting her husband's compliment. She'd been married to Jack for twenty-nine years of happiness and anxiety. Like countless times before, the pleasure of a dinner with her husband was offset by the knowledge that the cop would be going back to work following the meal. "What time is Leo coming by?"

Jack grabbed the serving tray with the meatloaf to help Natalie clear the table. He shook his head and smiled. "We've just got to follow up on something. It shouldn't take long. He'll be here in about a half hour. Really, we won't be long tonight."

Leo arrived on time and the two METs headed into Boston, feeling a rush like athletes feel just before a big game. They were, after all, going into the Combat Zone to intentionally annoy a major Mob figure in Boston. Jack wanted to turn the screws on Joe Vito. Now that the FBI had his back, Jack was confident he could take chances, as long as they weren't extreme or foolish.

Once they arrived at the Zone, Leo parked the car, partially blocking an alley beside Club 77. While Jack held the traffic for him, he backed into the alley so the car was facing out to the street for an easy exit. It was a few minutes before eight o'clock, so the Club wouldn't be very crowded yet. Time to get started.

Music was playing as Jack and Leo walked in, but the dance platform was empty. Most of the patrons paid no attention to the two men, but Big Ted stood up straight and eyed them as they approached the bar. He didn't know them, and he instinctively thought *cop*. Leo and Jack were impressed with the man's great height.

"You guys want something?"

"Now, now," said Leo. "That's not a very customer-friendly tone of voice."

"So far you haven't ordered a drink, so you aren't customers yet," snapped Big Ted.

"Well, we don't want drinks, big fella." Leo flipped out his police badge. "We want to talk to your boss, Joe Vito. Where can we find him?"

Big Ted put both hands on the bar and leaned toward Leo. "Mr. Vito's not in, so why don't you get lost?"

Jack looked around and saw many very young-looking people in the bar. "You know, big guy, you've got a lot of young faces in this place."

"They're grad students from Harvard and MIT. They're doing research."

"Well, maybe we'll just check their student IDs. If just one of them turns out to be underage, we'll shut the place down and haul him and you off in the paddy wagon. I bet Mr. Vito would love that."

Big Ted stood back from the bar and relaxed his threatening posture. "Oh, I forgot. He said he was going to be in his office for a while. It's over there."

He pointed toward the office, and the MET cops walked in that direction. As soon as they'd turned, Big Ted reached for the bar phone, pushed the intercom button and alerted Joe Vito about his visitors.

Jack knocked on the office door and waited. He was about to knock again when the door opened. Joe Vito stood in the doorway and looked the two men up and down. "What can I do for you gentlemen?"

"Are you Joe Vito?" asked Leo, holding up his badge.

"That's right. Is there a problem?"

"I'm Detective Contino and this is Detective Barbado. There was a big problem a few weeks ago, Joe. Four men were gunned down at a card game in the North End. We understand that you were pals with them."

"I read about that in the paper. Too bad. I think I met Di Nardi once or twice, and Senatori, too. I wouldn't exactly call them pals. It's a shame there's so much violence in this city. You officers need to crack down on it so we businessmen can feel safe here."

Joe walked back into his office, followed by Jack and Leo. He gestured for them to sit, but they declined. Vito, also remained standing and offered the men a drink, which they also declined.

"This is a pretty good business you've got here," said Jack, looking around the room. "You've got a big bar, a very big bartender, live music, dancing girls. You must do all right."

"I make a living."

"Well, that living must be getting better since you're taking over Di Nardi's, that guy you met once or twice," said Jack.

The smirk left Joe Vito's face. "Who told you that?"

"Word on the street," said Jack.

Vito paused before speaking again. "Some of us business owners on the street decided to pitch in and help keep the place running after the owner's death." He had confidence in his comeback. "We figure it's good for business. We don't want to see a place get run down. We'll have our lawyers straighten out the title to the place when his estate is settled."

Jack and Leo looked at each other. There could be some truth to Vito's answer. "I'm sure you will," said Leo, "being such dedicated businessmen and all. We understand that one of those other concerned business people is a guy named Ben Secani."

Jack looked directly at Vito.

Joe was now getting annoyed, to Jack's pleasure. "Is that all you guys came here for, to talk about Di Nardi's unfortunate death and how we're keeping his place going?"

"You know him, don't you?"

"Ben Secani? Oh, yeah, I know him. He does some odd jobs for me now and then."

"Yeah, I'll bet he does," said Leo. "I'll bet he's a real handyman."

Jack continued to stare down Joe Vito. "We have reason to believe he was at that card game, but somehow managed to survive the unfortunate violence." He waited for Vito's reply.

"I wouldn't know anything about that. What a guy does in his spare time is his own business. Why don't you go talk to him?"

"We'll do that. Since he works for you, you must have an address and home phone for the guy."

Joe said nothing. He just sat behind his desk and flipped through his Rolodex. He scribbled Ben's contact information on a piece of paper and gave it to Jack. "Have a good time. Now, if you two don't mind, I've got a business to run here."

"Sure," said Leo. "Thanks for the nice chat. Too bad we can't stay for the dancing girls."

Smiling, Jack and Leo walked back to the alley where they had left the car. "I thought that went well, Jack, didn't you?"

"Absolutely. I always enjoy talking with the local businessmen of the community. They're so civic-minded."

Leo poked Jack on the arm as they walked. "I'll bet you he's on the phone to Secani right now."

Jack nodded. "And that's a phone call being recorded by our friends at the Bureau." Jack was pleased with the situation. They got in their car, and Leo eased it out onto the street. "Take me home, partner," said Jack. "We're done for the night."

*****

Leo was right about Joe Vito's next phone call. He dialed Di Nardi's where he expected Ben to be. He picked up after three rings. "Hello. Ben Secani."

"Ben, get over here right away."

"Hey, what's going on, boss?"

"That cop, Contino, was just here. He was here with another cop. Get over here pronto. We need to talk."

Joe was so agitated that he poured himself a shot of Scotch and knocked it down. He paced the floor for a while and then had another drink. It seemed like an eternity before Ben showed up in his office. He was breathing heavily after jogging the three blocks from Di Nardi's to Club 77.

"Sit down, Ben. We've got a problem, and we have to take care of it."

Ben knew not to make any remarks that could be misconstrued. He had never seen Joe so unglued. "Ben, tell me again exactly why you brought that girl over here last Sunday."

Ben took a moment to collect his thoughts. "When I went over to her place, she seemed fine. The money was all there and she got real hot in bed. She did me like she never did before. After, she started talking about the two of us getting away some weekend. I didn't go for it, so she started asking about my businesses and the people I work with. She wanted to see the Zone. So I figured the coolest thing would be to play along with her. It was a Sunday afternoon, so I knew there wouldn't be much to see, so I decided to satisfy her curiosity right then. We drove by Di Nardi's and came over here."

Joe listened carefully. "What did you tell her about Di Nardi's?"

"I said I owned ten percent of it and she asked who owned the rest, so I told her. I guess I was bragging a little bit."

Joe shook his head without saying anything. Ben got the message and looked away, realizing he had made a mistake. Vito changed the subject quickly. "Those cops know I took over Di Nardi's. How?"

"Maybe it was Morelli."

"No, not Morelli. It's more likely those cops are talking to the girl. You said she's never pried into your business before. Now, she is. There's got to be a reason." Joe Vito's tone was firm. He leaned back in his chair, and a calm came over him as if he had just found a clearing in the woods.

"Joe, are you sure?"

"There's one way to be sure. Take a couple of guys and go sweep her apartment for bugs."

Ben was startled, but kept quiet. Then Joe leaned on his desk, looking straight at Ben. "Look, I know you go way back with this kid, but she's gotten involved with our business now. If she's talking to the cops, Ben, there's only one way out for us."

Ben got up from his chair and walked toward the door. He knew he couldn't save Maria if she was informing the cops. If he tried, then he'd be a dead man. His lifelong feelings for Maria made it hurt, but he knew he had no choice.

Ben took two men with him to the apartment. One man was short and heavyset. The other was average height and ruggedly built. The short man had a small black tool pouch hanging from his belt. They went in through the front door and walked calmly up the stairs.

Ben gave directions to the man with the tools before they got inside. "There are phones in the living room and the bedroom. Check them both while we look in other places. We'll check for wires coming from behind wall hangings, bookcases, tables—everything. A wire usually leads to a microphone."

The short man went about dismantling the living room phone while Ben and the other man came up empty. Then the short man waved to Ben. He had unscrewed the mouthpiece from the handset and there was the bug, a simple tap system microphone. "Boy, those FBI guys aren't very sophisticated," he whispered to Ben, just in case the room was bugged. "These things are piss poor. They often cause feedback, which is easy to detect. I guess they figured this user wouldn't notice."

The short man reassembled the phone, then checked the bedroom and found phone bug number two. Ben and his partner found nothing. They straightened up and left quickly. Ben had to get back to Joe Vito. He wished he didn't.

When Ben got back to Club 77, he went straight to Joe's office. Joe was seated at his desk. He looked up at Ben and waved his hand across his mouth, a signal not to talk. Joe was taking no chances. He motioned with his little finger for Ben to follow him. They walked out into the hallway and headed to a back exit from the building. They stepped out into an alley wide enough for delivery trucks to enter and leave. Joe let the door close behind them and they stood on a short loading platform with a pipe railing.

Joe looked at Ben, but didn't speak. Ben knew the question without having to hear it. He wet his lips quickly before speaking. "We found bugs in both her phones, nothing else."

Joe looked down and shook his head. "That cuts it, Ben. She's talking to the cops. They've probably confronted her in person and grilled her. Then they put bugs on her phones to try to get more. If they know about her hooking for you, then they must have made a deal with her. She digs into your affairs and tells them what she learns. That's how they knew about me taking over Di Nardi's place. Now it adds up."

Ben gritted his teeth. He knew what Joe was going to say next.

"You've got to take her out. Do it right away and do it carefully."

Chapter Twenty-Five

Martin took Maria to dinner in Hillsboro and then drove back to his house, all the while anticipating the upcoming weekend trip to Massachusetts. He hadn't looked forward to a weekend with such emotion since he was in college. He hoped he could concentrate on teaching his Friday classes without the distraction. *Be patient,* he told himself.

Maria looked at Martin as they drove back to Henniker. "Martin, I really need to go back to my apartment tonight. I've got some work to finish, and I'd like to get packed for the weekend."

Martin was disappointed to hear this from her, but he understood. She was right. Besides, they'd have the next few days together, finally.

"I understand, Maria," he said. "Okay, get your work done and get ready for tomorrow. We can leave from my office in the afternoon. If we go around five, we could stop for dinner in Manchester. That would allow for the rush hour traffic to subside by the time we reach greater Boston. We'll do better to drive around Boston rather than try to go straight through the city and wind up on the Southeast Expressway."

"I agree. That sounds like a good plan."

They pulled into the lot behind The Inn where Maria had left her car, and he parked beside it. She slid out of the passenger seat while fishing in her coat pocket for her keys. Martin walked quickly around his car to reach her. He took her in his arms and squeezed her tightly, then he kissed her. "This is going to be a great weekend," he said, still holding her.

"Yes, it is. I'll see you in class tomorrow."

Martin released her and stepped back as she got into her car and backed out of the driveway. Tomorrow seemed too far away for him.

Maria's mood changed quickly as she drove back to her apartment. She still didn't know how she was going to deal with Ben this weekend. She was determined to go away with Martin, however. But what possible excuse could she come up with to cancel whatever Ben would have set up for her?

Once at her apartment, Maria decided the best thing she could do was to bury herself in her homework. She had a chapter to read in her Economics text and some lecture notes to type up, as well. Her mind was well-focused on her work for over an hour, and she kept Ben Secani out of her thoughts. Then the phone rang.

Maria was startled at first. She wasn't sure if she should answer it or not. If it was Ben, she wasn't prepared with an excuse for the weekend. She let it ring. *No. It could be Martin.* After five rings, she answered it.

"Maria, it's Ben," said the voice after Maria spoke a soft greeting.

"Oh, hello Ben." Her heart sank.

"Something's come up," he said. "I've got to see you right away, tonight."

"Tonight?" she cried. "Ben, it's late. I've got studying to do and an early class tomorrow. I can't come to Boston tonight. Can't it wait?"

"No, Maria, it can't wait. You get your ass down here right now. Do you want me to come after you and make some noise in your little college town?"

"No, no, don't do that. I'll come. I'll meet you at the apartment in about ninety minutes. Can't you at least tell me what this is all about?"

"No, not over the phone. Just get here!" Then he hung up.

Maria felt sick to her stomach. Why was he so angry? Could he have found out about her talking to Jack Contino? Her plans for the weekend with Martin were gone. There was no way she could avoid Ben. Tears filled Maria's eyes as she stood by her phone.

She knew she couldn't just disappear when Martin was expecting to take her with him, so she decided to go back to his office to tell him. But tell him what? She'd have to think of something quickly.

Martin heard the entrance door to the building open followed by footsteps on the stairs. He was stunned to see Maria enter his office.

"Maria! What is it? Is something wrong?"

"I'm sorry, Martin, but something's come up. I have to leave for Boston right away. I can't go with you tomorrow."

"What? Maria, I don't understand. Just an hour ago you were happy and excited about the upcoming trip. Now this. What's going on?"

"Nothing's going on. It's just something with the family business in Boston. That's all."

"What do you mean that's all? Look, I've tried to be understanding about this family business you have, especially since you said you don't have a family anymore. So what is it that's got such a hold on you?"

"Martin, please!"

"I love you, Maria. I want you to be with me and I hoped you wanted that, too."

"I do, Martin, I do. You've got to believe me."

"Then give up this Boston thing and go away with me."

The tears began to flow from Maria's eyes. "I can't, Martin. I just can't. I'll call you when I get back."

She turned and fled down the stairs and out the building. She ran to her car, got in and started the engine. Martin was right behind her. He rapped his knuckles on the window, but Maria wouldn't open it. She locked the door.

"Maria, stop. Don't do this, please."

Maria didn't answer. She just sped out of the parking lot, leaving the bewildered Martin standing alone. He watched as she drove away. He wanted to follow her, but knew she was already too far ahead. He had no idea where in Boston she was headed.

*****

The door to the building opened while Martin stood dazed by what had just happened. A lone figure stepped out. "You okay, Professor?"

Martin was startled by the voice of Officer Mills, who passed through The Inn while making his rounds. He had heard part of the exchange between Martin and Maria.

"Yes, Jerry. I'm fine."

"You got a funny way of showing it. Wasn't that a student who just left in a hurry?"

"Yes, yes, Maria Falcone. She was . . . upset about a grade I gave her on a paper."

"Hmmm, I see. What did she get?"

"Get? Oh, her grade. A *B*. I gave her a *B*. She usually gets *A*s, so she was upset a bit."

"A bit." Wow! I hope she never gets a *C*."

"Yes. Well, I'll just go up and close my office. Good night, Jerry."

"Goodnight, Professor."

Chapter Twenty-Six

Ben found a parking space two blocks away from Maria's building on the same side of the street and walked back, checking the street as he walked. There was nothing out of the ordinary, as far as he could tell, so he let himself in to Maria's apartment. For years this had been his pleasure house, but there would be no pleasure here tonight. Ben dropped his coat over a chair and went into the kitchen to pour a drink. He carried his drink with him back into the living room, placed it on a table and closed the curtains at all the windows. Then he sat back in a chair and sipped his drink while contemplating how the rest of the night would play out.

Ben had never been troubled at doing his work before, no matter what the task, but this was different. How could have his life with Maria Falcone come to this? It didn't seem real that this had to be the last night of her life. But that was what the boss had decreed and there was no way out. His emotions ran from sadness to anger.

The sound of a key unlocking the apartment door awakened Ben from the light sleep that had overtaken him in his chair. He sat up with a start and wiped his face with both hands, then he stood up just before Maria emerged through the doorway and into the living room.

"Hello, Ben," she said as she took off her coat.

He didn't reply, but just stood still, his arms folded across his chest.

There was no warm greeting, no hugs or kisses this time.

"Hello," she said. "What's so important that you had to drag me down here tonight?" she asked, a slight crack in her voice.

"Have a seat," ordered Ben.

Maria sat on the end of the sofa, and Ben sat down in a chair near her. "Last weekend," he started, "you said you wanted us to get away for a while. Then you asked about my business and the people I work for. Why?"

Maria pressed her hands together before speaking. "Ben, I told you, we could both benefit from a change of pace sometimes and I still think so. But you didn't agree. So I thought that if I couldn't get you away from your world sometimes, maybe I could be a part of it."

"You are a part of it."

"I know." Maria's mind was racing trying to build an excuse. She turned her head away and then looked back at him. "But this life is getting frustrating, Ben! Every weekend, I come to town and go out with some rich John who wants to get laid. It's getting to be too much, Ben!"

"Too much?" snapped Ben. "You mean that healthy bank account of yours is too much? This apartment is too much. Is your car too much?"

Maria squirmed in her chair. "You don't understand me, Ben. You're not the one who has to climb in bed with these strangers."

"Hey, you came to me with this idea. What did you call it . . . unconventional business. It seems to me you've been very successful with it."

Maria had no reply.

Ben sat up straight in his chair and looked at Maria. "I didn't tell you to come here so we could have a discussion about this. Maria, I know you had a visit from the MET police. I want you to tell me about it."

Maria went pale and swallowed hard. "How did you know that?"

"Never mind how I know. I know a lot of things. Tell me about it."

Maria rubbed her hands together as she tried to talk. "They were here the last time Mr. Sullivan took me out. They were waiting when he brought me home."

"What were they waiting for?"

Maria didn't know how to answer.

"They didn't arrest you, Maria. They didn't arrest Sullivan, either. They even let you keep the money Sullivan gave you, even though it's from an illegal enterprise. Why did they do that, Maria? Why did they let you and Sullivan off the hook?"

Maria felt her chest tighten and had trouble breathing. She couldn't talk, so Ben did the talking for her. "They wanted information from you, Maria. They think you know things that can help them, don't they?"

Maria nodded affirmatively as tears appeared in her eyes.

"They think you know things about me, don't they Maria?"

"But I don't know anything," she cried. "I mean, I couldn't tell them anything because you don't tell me anything about your business. You made that clear with me right from the beginning. I didn't tell them anything!"

"No, you didn't. You couldn't. So they told you to find out things. They told you to learn more about me. That's why you wanted me to take you into the Zone and meet my boss."

Maria was near panic. "What could I do, Ben? They could arrest me. I could go to jail. Prison! What was I supposed to do? What was I . . ."

Ben took a seat beside her, reaching out for her hands. "It's going to be okay. We're going to go talk to Joe. He knows how to handle the cops. He'll tell us exactly what we need to do." He needed to get her out of the building and set her up for the finish.

r r r r

Leo pulled up along the curb in front of Jack's house after their visit to Joe Vito's club. "Nice work tonight, partner," he said, as Jack worked his big frame out of the car. He planted his feet and turned, twisting his body to face his partner. "I think this will start shaking things in Mr. Vito's organization. It should bring Ben Secani to the surface. Thanks for the ride."

"No sweat. See you . . . hey, looks like somebody's glad you're home." Leo pointed to Natalie coming out of the house and down the walk toward her husband. "Hope she's not pissed that we stopped for a couple of cold ones."

"What?" Jack turned away from Leo, confused by his wife's sudden appearance.

"Jack, I'm so glad you're finally home," said Natalie. She paused a minute to catch her breath. "You got a phone call a while ago from a man at New Sussex College in New Hampshire. He tried your office phone first but couldn't reach you. He said you told him to call you if he saw or heard anything strange or unusual happening regarding a student named Maria Falcone."

"Okay. Okay. What was his name?"

"He said he was a Security guard . . . ah . . . Mills, Jerry Mills. He left his number."

"Okay. Thanks, hon. Leo, you better come inside."

They all went into the house and stood in the entryway, where a phone sat on a small table against the wall. The table had a seat on it for callers, but Jack just stood beside it. He dialed the number Officer Mills had left. It was his office phone at the college. The female voice of the night dispatcher answered.

"Hello, New Sussex College, Office of Security. How can I help you?"

"This is Detective Jack Contino with the MDC Police in Boston. I'm returning a call from Officer Mills. I need to speak with him."

"He's out on his rounds right now. If you like, I can try to reach him on his radio."

"Yes, please do that."

The woman put Jack on hold and his line seemed dead for a moment. Then her voice came back on the line. "Hello, sir?"

"Yes, yes. I'm here."

"Officer Mills isn't responding on his radio. He must be away from his car. I'll keep trying him, but this may take a while. Can you give me your number so he can call you back once I reach him?"

"Yes, of course."

Jack gave the dispatcher his phone number and hung up. His face showed his frustration at not being able to get through to Officer Mills, and he began to pace the floor.

Leo stood against the opposite wall with his arms crossed in front of him. "What do you think, Jack?"

"I have no idea, but I don't like it."

A few minutes before, Jack and Leo had felt they were getting control of the situation. They put the squeeze on

Joe Vito and were sure it would start some wheels turning. Maybe the wheels were turning too fast.

Natalie made some coffee for the men and brought it out to them near the phone. They thanked her, and she went back into the living room.

"I'd better make some room for this first," said Leo. Jack nodded as Leo walked down the hall to the half bath just off the kitchen. When he returned, Jack was still pacing and his coffee cup sat on the table. Then Jack went down the hall.

Nearly twenty minutes went by before the phone finally rang. Jack grabbed it. "Hello."

"Hello Detective, this is Jerry Mills at New Sussex College. How you doing?"

"Fine. Fine. What's going on?"

Officer Mills was dismayed by Jack's abruptness. The friendliness of their first meeting was gone.

"Well, you said I should call you if something strange happened. I was doing my rounds in the Administration Building earlier when I heard Professor Martin and that Falcone girl in his office. Their voices were getting loud and she seemed to be crying. She stormed out of the place with him right behind her. She got in her car and tooled on out of the parking lot in a big hurry. I saw him try to stop her, but he couldn't catch up. I asked him if everything was okay and he gave me some cock and bull story about her being upset about her grade on a paper. I knew that was baloney because I overheard her say something about having to go to Boston right away. He didn't seem to want her to go. She said something came up suddenly. Whatever it was, it sure got them both in a bad way."

"Jerry, when did she leave?"

"About an hour and a quarter, maybe twenty, minutes. She should be in town about now."

"Thanks, Jerry."

"Sure. No problem." Jerry was talking to a dead phone.

Natalie Contino watched as her husband and his partner rushed out of the house and into the night. They left the front door open in their haste, so she walked up to it and closed it slowly. She had seen Jack and Leo leave the house to tend to police matters many times before, but this time it was especially unsettling to her.

Jack pulled out the slip of paper with Ben Secani's address on it, as Leo drove away from Jack's house. "We headed for Secani's place or the girl's apartment?"asked Leo.

"The apartment. It sounds like Secani has called her down to Boston in a hurry. If I'm right, she could be in big trouble. I'll send someone over to his place to see if he's still there, just in case."

Jack got on the car radio and told the dispatcher to send a unit over to the address he read from the slip of paper in his hand. His instructions were emphatic. *Do not apprehend.* Just find out if Secani is there and report back. Jack put the flashing light on the roof of the car and turned on the siren. They had to drive quickly.

A second radio call from Jack and another MET unit was sent over to Maria's Back Bay apartment. The order was to go in quietly and wait a block west of the address.

Leo drove out of Somerville into Cambridge via College Avenue and Day Streets, then down Route 2A, Massachusetts Avenue. They went through the MIT campus and over the Harvard Bridge, where Jack killed the light and siren, then into the Back Bay and on to Marlborough Street. Just before reaching Maria's block, they got the radio call telling them there was nobody at Ben Secani's place.

The MET black and white car was there waiting for them as Jack and Leo approached. They each rolled down their windows as Leo pulled his car up beside the patrol car. Jack leaned forward and spoke to the uniformed officers. "We don't want to be spotted from the front window, so we'll pull up a little closer and stop."

After driving up a little closer, the four METs approached the building on foot. There was a street light just outside the building and a light over the front entry. Jack ordered Leo and the driver of the black and white to cover the rear of the building, where a fire escape could be an exit for Secani. Jack and his colleague waited a half minute for the others to get in place before they started their approach. It was a cold night and, fortunately, the street was empty of pedestrians.

Jack was walking slowly and trying to decide the best way to enter the building. Should they hold back or go storming in? Either way could jeopardize Maria.

The decision was made for him when the door to the building opened and a man and woman came out. It was Secani and Maria. Ben was standing between the METs and Maria, holding her right arm with his left hand. His right arm hung down with his hand in his coat pocket.

Maria saw them first. "Oh no," she cried, as they reached the bottom step. Ben snapped his head in their direction. He swiftly pulled his weapon from his pocket and instinctively shot at the police uniform twice. The officer went down before he could draw his service revolver. Ben turned his aim toward Jack and fired. The big detective stepped to his right just before the shot hit him in the midsection, left side and he dropped to one knee and then the other. Maria screamed again and pulled away from Ben and dove between two parked cars at the curb. Ben fired a shot in her direction. That move was the break Jack needed. It gave him time to draw his revolver. In the most crucial moment of his life, Jack Contino kneeled on the sidewalk, blood streaming from his wound, vision beginning to fade, and fired one shot into the head of Ben Secani. Then he collapsed.

Leo and the other uniformed MET came running to the front of the building. "Oh, shit!' cried Leo. He rushed to his partner. As he did, Jack groaned and began to turn over onto his right side. "You better get me an ambulance, Leo. This thing hurts!"

"My partner's dead," said the uniformed MET, after checking the others. "So's Secani. The girl's been hit in the leg, but she's okay. I'll get on the radio."

Leo took off his coat and put it beneath Jack's head, then took out his handkerchief and held it against Jack's wound, applying pressure to slow the bleeding. "You still with me, Jack?"

"Yeah, I'm here. Don't worry, partner, I'm not going anywhere."

"Damned right, you're not. There's going to be a pile of paperwork on this case. You're not going to leave it all to me, pal."

Jack laughed and coughed at the same time. "Don't make me laugh, Leo. That smarts."

The uniformed officer lifted Maria off the street and carried her to his vehicle, helping her into the backseat. She was grazed in the back upper part of her left leg. The officer tended to it with a first aid kit from his glove compartment. It would do until the ambulance arrived.

Tears were flowing down Maria's face, but she summoned the strength to speak. "Is the detective dead?"

"No, Miss, but he's hurt pretty badly. He's quite a guy. He took that bullet and still managed to get the shooter. He saved your life, Miss. I sure hope he makes it."

"Me, too, officer. Me too."

Epilogue

Three years had passed since Jack was shot by Ben Secani. He'd survived the wound that just missed shattering his spleen, which would have been fatal. He lost a lot of blood as it was, and a smaller man might have died. But Jack Contino was a big, tough S.O.B. by his own admission and he wasn't ready to leave Natalie and the kids.

Shortly after he recovered and was ready for active duty once again, Jack decided to retire from police work. He was given a big retirement party and many honors, including personally signed letters of commendation from the Mayor of Boston, the Governor of the Commonwealth of Massachusetts and the Director of the Federal Bureau of Investigation. Still, he was troubled.

No charges were ever filed against Maria, because Jack saw to it that she was granted immunity as a police informant, provided she gave up her Boston enterprise. She went back to New Sussex College and began the process of healing with Martin Douglas. Joe Vito got off free. There wasn't enough evidence to link him to the Mob massacre, especially with Ben Secani dead. Ben's boss couldn't make a move toward Maria without throwing suspicion on himself, so she was safe. It burned Jack up to see Vito skate away, but Vito was not his problem anymore.

There was still the issue of Tommy Shea, who had grown into a major threat and had made it to the FBI's Most Wanted list. That's what bothered Jack the most: the fact that the Bureau could appear to be hunting Shea while giving him protection at the same time. Jack wanted to see that changed.

One spring day while walking in his neighborhood, Jack passed the local Boys and Girls Club, where he'd often volunteered his time, and saw a gray-haired man trimming some flowers in the flower bed in front of the building. It was Bill Tanner, a retired MET cop Jack knew from his early days on the force. Bill waved and said "Hello Jack," as he passed by.

Jack returned the wave and continued walking and then stopped. He went back to Bill.

Before Jack could talk, Bill asked, "Are you okay, Jack? You look like something's bothering you."

Jack searched for words. "Bill, it's the murder case I was involved in a couple of years ago. Maybe you can help with something that's been bothering me."

"Well, I'll try, Jack," he replied. "What is it?"

"The young woman, Maria Falcone, She was a snitch, an informant," he said, holding his head down as if in confession. "I was using her to get at Ben Secani. I knew he was a killer, but I couldn't prove it. Somehow, Secani found out about it and he tried to kill her before she could help me. I put her in harm's way and almost got her killed. And a good young cop did get killed in the shoot-out. You know, I never killed a man in all my years of police work. I sometimes wonder if I went about it the right way."

Bill Tanner looked at Jack compassionately. "Jack, you're a decent man and an outstanding police officer. Everybody says so. Police work is very hard. I know that from experience. You have to make many hard decisions. Trying to use Maria Falcone as a snitch, even though you knew it would put her in danger, was such a decision." Jack nodded.

"Tell me this, Jack," said Bill. "Ben Secani was a professional killer, wasn't he?" Jack nodded again. "He killed those Mob guys. He killed that young MET and he almost killed you and the girl. If you didn't get him, Jack, he would have killed you, the girl and more people in the future?"

He watched Jack's head move up and down in affirmation. "You killed him in self-defense and defending the girl and your colleagues. It seems to me, Jack, that your decision to use Maria Falcone was justified and you saved her from Secani, who was going to kill her, sure as anything. And he would have killed more people in the future."

Jack lifted his head up and looked at the Bill's face. Those words carried truth in them that began to make Jack feel better.

"I believe you did the right thing, Jack."

Jack reached out his big hand, and Bill took it. Then Jack clasped his other hand over Bill's. He didn't shake the hand. He simply squeezed it gently, holding on for a moment. "I can live with that," said Jack gratefully. He released Bill's hand and resumed his stroll down the neighborhood sidewalk. It was a good day.

THE END

About the Author

Steve Marini holds a Master's degree in Educational Technology from Boston University and a B.A. in Business Administration from New England College and has spent over thirty years in the Education/Training field, including posts in higher education and the federal government.

Although he describes himself as a "card carrying New Englander," he lived for twenty-six years in Maryland while pursuing a career spanning four federal agencies. His background has enabled him to serve as a project manager at the National Security Agency, the Environmental Protection Agency, the National Fire Academy and the Centers for Medicare and Medicaid Services, where he worked with teams of experts in various fields to develop state-of-the-art training for both classrooms and distance learning technologies.

A "Baby Boomer," Steve has taken up fiction writing as he moved into his career final frontier. Married for thirty-six years, a father of three and a grandfather, Steve and his wife Louise own a home on Cape Cod that will serve as his private writer's colony for the years ahead.

BLOG: http://babyboomerspm.blogspot.com/
FACEBOOK: http://www.facebook.com/StevenPMarini

CPSIA information can be obtained
at www.ICGtesting.com
Printed in the USA
FFOW03n2031221014
8271FF